To Kyle!

fuorimano

Prima edizione maggio 2010

Dario Castagno

An Osteria in Chianti

a novel

BARBERA EDITORE

An Osteria in Chianti

To the loving memory of Mary Herczog

1908

The year was inaugurated by the first-ever New Year's Eve ball drop in New York's Times Square; a year which would see Mother's Day celebrated internationally for the first time, and in which the Olympic Games were to be marred by dispute.

In England, Lord Baden-Powell founded the Boy Scouts. An egocentric Englishman, Harry Bensley, departed from Trafalgar Square pushing a pram and wearing an iron mask, with the goal of completing a tour of the world on foot.

In Portugal, a deranged assassin killed King Carlos I and his heir, Prince Luis Filipe. A Frenchman named Farman piloted the first flight with passengers.

In America, the Republican William Howard Taft won the presidential election, and the Federal Bureau of Investigation, or FBI, was founded. Henry Ford conceived the Model T, and a man named Thomas Selfridge became the first victim of an air disaster.

Farther afield, Butch Cassidy and the Sundance Kid were killed in Bolivia, and Pu Yi became Emperor of China at the age of two.

In Italy, a young monarchy was in quest of a distinct national identity. King Victor Emanuel III appointed Prime Minister Giovanni Giolitti to his third term as head of the government. And 200,000 Sicilians perished in a dramatic earthquake in Messina.

The Palio of Siena of the 2nd of July was postponed to the following day due to rain, and was won by the Noble Contrada dell'Oca (Goose) with the exacta Morella mounted by Picino. The Palio of the 16th of August was won by the Contrada Valdimontone (Ram) with the same horse, mounted this time by the jockey Nappa.

According to the Coptic calendar, 1908 was 1624; for the Koreans, 4241; for the Thais, 2451. In the Islamic calendar it was 1325; in the Persian, 1286; and in the Holocene calendar it would be 11908. For the Hindus it was 1963; for the Shaka Sanvat, it was 1830; for the Kali Yuga, it was 5009; and for the Jews, 5668. The Ethiopians referred to it as 1900; the Chinese, 4605-6; the Byzantines, 7416; the Burhams, 1270; the Buddhists, 2452; the Berbers, 2858; and the Baha' i', 64. In the Gregorian calendar it was MCMVIII.

The year saw the births of Herbert von Karajan, Betty Davis, Henry Cartier, Luc Bresson, Simone de Beauvoir, Oskar Schindler, Max Grundig, James Stewart, Ian Fleming, Salvador Allende, Simon Wiesenthal, and a child baptized in a modest chapel in Chianti who was given the name Ultimo Gori.

Chapter 1

September 2008

As I pedaled through the upper hills of Chianti, I couldn't help being enraptured by the extraordinary variations of light that shimmered between the rows of grapevines.

In just a few weeks the countryside would undergo a profound metamorphosis. The ardent carmine of the flora would dull to straw-like yellow, and the fallen leaves would blanket the steep, rocky terrain until, inevitably, they would be carried away by the wind. Then the bare winter aspect of the vines, drawn up in regimented rows, would bring to mind the crosses in the military cemetery I had just left behind.

The previous day I had fervently followed the on-road world cycling championship, which was won against all odds by an unknown Italian, Alessandro Ballan. The young victor crossed the finish line alone, arms raised in triumph, riding a bicycle manufactured by Wilier Triestina that was identical to the one I possessed. During the solemn prize ceremony, I had jumped up and down in ecstasy on the sofa while balancing a terracotta cup filled to the brim with a *prosecco* of no special value; it sloshed over onto the divan cover. In a fit of patriotism, I held the cup high for the Italian National Anthem, the *Inno di Mameli*, then downed its contents in one gulp.

The make of Ballan's bicycle had been the main stimulus for my current tour; clad head to toe in biking gear, I had proudly steered my new and prestigious Triestina over the steep roads that unwind through Chianti, and with increasing fatigue was coming now to the end. The extravagant aftertaste of Ballan's victory inspired me to pump the pedals more energetically than normal as I headed uphill, and I continued to do so as I came over the top, launching myself downwards along the hairpin curbs with wild buoyancy. My head bobbed low between the handlebars; my body was curved in an aerodynamic arc; and I plunged on with a dynamism I thought I'd long lost.

Summer had ended and the days were fresher and pleasanter, the sky more frequently covered with nimbus clouds burgeoning with the first rainfalls of the fall. This morning, however, the sky was clear and the air was saturated with the sweet, mawkish must of the harvest. These were the first days of the *vendemmia*, and the vineyards were teeming with grape pickers stripping from the vines the succulent bounty of mature fruit that the *cantinieri* were about to transform into the precious nectar of Bacchus.

I filled my lungs with these fragrant scents of the October countryside; at the same time my eyes drank in the suggestive beauties of the territory. And at the very moment that my brain was archiving them, its prince of products, the wine (which I had abundantly abused over the past few days due to the annual feast in honor of the *vendemmia*) mixed with the blood now pumping so forcefully through my veins. And all at once I felt I was indeed an essential part of this splendid corner of the universe.

I braked and skidded to a halt. Dripping with sweat, I placed my world-champion bicycle in its usual place: leaning against the ancient kneading trough situated on the main wall of my living room.

At the end of a revitalizing shower, I bundled up into my spongy bathrobe, now grown coarse and abrasive due to the countless rough washings without any softener. As a typical single Latin male, I always ignored both the washing programs and water temperatures suggested by the user's manual. Yet I remained extremely fond of that bathrobe for a particularity that for me outweighed any consideration of comfort: it was decorated with the blue, yellow and green of my Contrada in Siena, the *Nobil Contrada del Bruco* (Caterpillar).

Worn out but satisfied by my cycling adventure, I now noticed that the red light of the answering machine was winking. I pressed the button with the right hand while I was rubbing my hair with the other. An unknown female voice, with an unsteady tone and a perceptible dose of emotion, informed me that Ultimo wasn't well. The voice requested I go without any hesitation to his home.

Restless and disturbed by the news I had just received, I instinctively reached for the effigy of the caterpillar sewn onto the robe's breast pocket, so close to my heart. While fiddling with the basting, my eyes drifted out of focus, and I conjured up Ultimo; not one single image in particular, but an idealization formed deep in the mysterious gorge of my reminiscence.

While still contemplating my friend, my gaze was attracted by a praying mantis that had reached the end of its vital cycle and was now lying on the terracotta tiles before the fireplace.

The anguished creature was distended on one side, and its asymmetric head looked up at me, its forelimbs united as if in appeal for my aid. It seemed to move in slow motion; this Tyrannosaurus Rex of the insect world, this bogey of grasshoppers, was now reduced to complete vulnerability, at the mercy of the world it once ruled. With a sudden start I rose, picked it up, and piteously deposited it on the vase filled with begonias on the window sill. Let it meet its fate, at least, under an open sky.

I then went to change into my usual jeans and a white shirt, with the intention of immediately visiting Ultimo.

Chapter 2

October 1983

During the drive to Ultimo's farmhouse, I chose to listen to Tchaikovsky's powerful first piano concerto for which I had a particular fondness. While the music swirled around me and the familiar Chianti scenarios streamed by the car windows, I pondered the circumstances of our first meeting.

Sometimes it seemed I met Ultimo by mere chance; others, that destiny had thrown us together. If the former, how fortuitous; if the latter, how like playthings we are, our lives subordinated to some generative power that has its wheels and cogs ever in motion, manipulating us like levers.

I was roughly seventeen years of age in that distant October of 1983 when I serenely propped my Vespa against the stone wall of an apparently long-unused barn that flanked an ancient farmhouse. There are many such husks scattered around the entire Chianti territory.

That morning I searched for mushrooms in a chestnut forest, returning hours later with a single miserable *porcino* in the wicker basket. When I reached the barn I saw incredulously that my scooter was no longer where I had left it.

Assaulted by sudden anxiety, I hurled my gaze in all directions until it fell upon an elderly man digging furrows with his spade in a small vegetable garden. He wore an ivory-colored woolen vest with one sleeve rolled up to his elbow and the other buttoned properly around his wrist. Shading his face was a wide-brimmed straw hat with a black ribbon band; his worn-out velvet corduroy trousers, the shade of Dijon mustard, were strapped to his skinny waist by a fraying leather belt. His tiny feet, which would have been the envy of a professional *calciatore* (soccer player), were tucked in cowhide leather boots, which were caked with dried mud.

Since he was apparently the sole person on hand, I approached him and asked if he had seen my *Vespina*. As I spoke, he continued his work with his head bent over and his back arched, completely ignoring my presence. When I finished my question he reluctantly hoisted his gaze and squinted as one does when the sun is too bright; but despite the squint I could see his vivacious, sprightly turquoise eyes.

He removed his hat, revealing a riot of snow-white hair that tumbled over a neck as slender as a stem, around which he had knotted a checkered blue cloth. On his cheek there glowed a deep, garish scar, like an island in the sea of his two-day beard. He seemed possessed of a well proportioned, trim, athletic body, lean and vigorous.

With a casual gesture he pulled the kerchief from his neck and dried the sweat from his forehead; then he blew his faintly pockmarked nose before replacing the cloth in his back pocket.

"Yes, I saw it," he said in a marked Tuscan accent, his delivery crisp and incisive. A curious smirk marred his mouth for an instant, and he propped himself on the wooden handle of the spade, which was still biting into the terrain; a pleasant, earthy odor wafted up from the soil he had just turned over. Then, supposing he had given me a suitable reply, he replaced his hat and continued calmly to dig his furrows.

I moved another step closer, swallowing nervously. "Excuse me," I said with the most polite tone of voice I could manage, "do you by any chance know where it is? I really do need to get back home now."

This time he responded with unmistakable bad grace, whirling on me and snarling, "It's on the tree!"

"On the tree? What tree?"

He jerked his thumb in the direction of an ancient mulberry.

I turned, and saw with astonishment my Vespa hanging halfway up the trunk, at exactly the point where the branches start to spread out. I was stupefied.

Before I had time to say anything, he rebuked me: "You were blocking the entrance to the barn where I store my tools, so I moved it. Now piss off, you can't stay here!"

"How on earth do you expect me to get it down?" I protested, feeling a slight swell of courage.

Teed off, he released the handgrip and threw the spade into the slushy vegetable garden. With a swinging gait he strode over to the tree; I followed with difficulty, trying to keep pace. Then he raised his arms, grabbed the scooter, and hauled it down as if it were no more than a sack of laundry.

I couldn't believe what I'd just witnessed. I had no idea whether I should thank him, or curse him, or get away as fast as my Vespa could carry me. Before I could decide, he broke the silence himself, nodding at the *porcino* I had collected.

"I hope you have no intention of eating that. It's baleful." He grinned. "It'll give you the shits." He snatched it from my basket and launched it into a tangled blackberry bush. "You youngsters are all the same. Listen, you must never fool around with mushrooms. Follow me."

I trotted along behind him, intrigued; he went up the stairs to the entrance of the very stone house I had been certain was uninhabited, then flung open the door and invited me inside.

A fragrance that reminded me of old drug stores hovered through the lodging: a heady combination of soaps, detergents, paints, provisions, and dust. In spite of myself, I felt comforted. The furniture was basic and blackened by time; set in the far wall were a wooden stove and a hearth thick with ashes that were still warm.

The old man led me to a counter where he produced a flask and two empty glasses. He filled both to the brim with red wine and wordlessly offered me one. Then he swallowed his own in one long guzzle and slammed the glass against the ancient walnut table. While I occupied myself with a succession of small sips, he poured himself a refill and after having guzzled it again in an Amen, once more thumped it down forcefully against the board.

Though a bit intimidated, I asked why he banged the glass with so much ardor. He eyed me curiously for a moment, as if assessing me, then scratched at the bristly white hairs on his chin and gave me a smile that might have been mischievous or challenging, or both, and declared: "When one drinks wine all the senses ought to enjoy some benefit. The mouth gets to savor the taste, the nose captures the bouquet, and the eye is enriched by the color. Why then should the ear be excluded?"

Delighted by this splendid response I raised my glass and pronounced, *"Magnifico!"* I extended my arm and introduced myself, expecting him to shake my hand and announce his own name in return. To my disappointment, he ignored my gesture completely. Instead he picked up three healthy looking *porcini* from a wicker basket on his mantelpiece and handed them to me with his calloused fingers covered in fresh mud.

"Eat them cooked in oil, two parsley leaves and a clove of garlic," he said. "Now go, you can't stay here."

He grabbed my arm, but with no friendly intention, and vigorously led me to the threshold where he ejected me with some force and slammed the door behind me. I was shaken by this bizarre and discourteous behavior. All I could do now was to hop on my scooter and leave, satisfied at any rate by the unexpected boon of *porcini* I had obtained *in extremis*.

I was about thirty kilometers from the village where I lived, which for us *Chiantigiani* is sufficient to make one a foreigner. In fact, when I stopped at a bar for a sandwich, the eyes of the regulars turned on me coldly, not recognizing or welcoming the longhaired youngster who had invaded their turf. But I sat down undaunted, and delivered my order.

Chapter 3

October 1983

My remembrance of that distant day in 1983 was interrupted by my approach to the farmhouse. I needed all my attention to maneuver my Fiat along the deserted, twisting roads so familiar to me, and yet so treacherously surprising. A small band of lizards was trying to absorb the warmth seeping up from the road, blissfully unaware of the danger of getting crushed underneath my tires. I swerved around them into the opposite lane, then back again; and my thoughts returned to Ultimo. Oddly I couldn't feel any inquietude for him. Perhaps it was the music, or the rapturous landscape in which I was fully submersed. The portents of fall were still feeble, but this wasn't unusual as all seasons arrive late in Chianti. From the window I could distinguish the many brilliant flowers still sprouting in the uncultivated fields: wild carrots, chicory and beautiful cyclamens whose pink buds appear even before the foliage. During the day the sun was still warm; at dusk however a chill settled in, serving notice that summer was indeed over.

As the fall colors blurred around me, my thoughts returned to 1983, and the episode that occurred in the bar.

I had ordered a *tramezzino* club sandwich stuffed with tuna and capers accompanied by a glass of Chianti Classico that I consumed while propped against the counter. The moment the bartender was disengaged, I asked if she was familiar with the old man who lived at the *podere Macie*: "The one with the scar."

The woman, whose hair was gathered in a lumpish nest tinted an obviously fake cinder blonde, contemplated me with a look sufficiently lacking in benevolence to announce that there was no hope of me having any kind of conversation with her. With a toss of her bogus-gold hair she did her best to dismiss me with a few disdainful syllables: that he was named Ultimo, that he rarely came to town, that he minded his own business, and finally, if I really had met him, I was lucky he hadn't shot me. I was sufficiently intelligent to read the emphasis she placed on the words "minds his own business," and so slipped 3200 Lire on the metal counter, pivoted on my heels and headed dejectedly towards the exit.

I passed a distinguished elderly gentlemen, clad in an extravagant double-breasted jacket. He was leafing through a newspaper provided for the bar's clientele, which by this time of day was already well used. He had undoubtedly overheard the entire exchange, and as I moved by him he lay down the crumpled *La Nazione* and blocked me at the exit, then politely requested to know the reason I had asked for information about Ultimo. He didn't possess a discernible Tuscan accent, characteristic of someone who had earned his living working the lands, but rather articulated his words in the manner of the landowning classes; there was also a peculiar formation to his vowels that seemed to indicate a period lived abroad.

He had a moustache so thick and bristly it looked like a horsehair brush seated on his upper lip; it was slightly moist from a glass of vermouth he had been sipping, and which now sat nearly empty on the table next to his felt hat (a Borsalino, I believe) and suede gloves. He ordered a second glass of Cinzano and a red wine, then invited me to make myself comfortable and removed his walking stick from the aluminum chair next to him. I sat down and related my encounter with Ultimo, trying not to omit any details. He listened thoughtfully while curling the ends of his moustache, his benevolent yet weary eyes seeming to drink in every word. When I finished he asked me what Ultimo looked like, if he seemed to me to be well. It was obvious that he somehow knew Ultimo, and equally so that it was many years since he had last seen him. Then he surprised me; he stood up with difficulty, grasped his walking stick and politely invited me to accompany him, arm in arm, outside.

With small strides due to his slow gait, he guided me towards an old Alfa Romeo. From his deep jacket pocket he produced a ring of keys, then flung open the passenger door and encouraged me to climb in. I was a bit hesitant, but my curiosity prevailed. With aristocratic élan he shut my door once I was comfortably seated, then took his place in the driver's seat, placed his hat and cane on the back seat, lit a cigar, inserted the keys and ignited the old car's engine; it started up at once. We drove through the town, past the main square, where an obelisk towered in the centre of a garden dedicated to the local victims of the Great War. He shifted down a couple gears, then applied the brakes, forcing the car to slow to a crawl. Once we were close to the monument, he opened the window using the hand crank.

"You see the two surnames carved there?" he said, darting his eyes in direction of the memorial. "Those were Ultimo's brothers." I was too far distant to be able to catch sight of them, but to please him I nodded in assent. Satisfied, he shifted into the third gear and the car nosed up slightly and left the square. Minutes later we were in the open countryside.

Chapter 4

October 1983

The sophisticated *signore* hastily flicked the still-glowing cigar from the window with a huff, then cleared his throat and launched into a lengthy explanation.

"Ultimo is the son of Gosto Gori and Annita Soccini," he said, "and first saw the light of day on the second of July, 1908, in a humble farmhouse in the Chianti Senese. There his family had dwelt for many generations, toiling in the fields as if suspended in time—a kind of twilight zone. The centuries flew by them as unremarkably as the seasons. Chianti is a paradoxical land, so capable of cultivating artists and poets, navigators and statesman, a whole society in miniature, and yet it is its multitude of minor personages who represent it most faithfully. And so, Ultimo.

"On that second of July, the leaden mugginess of summer was interrupted by a downpour so fierce that the Palio was canceled in nearby Siena; the central piazza was more suited to a boat race than a horserace. Yet the squall refreshed the air and released the pleasing scent of drenched earth, and such was the first breath Ultimo ever took. The community of farmers saw nothing exceptional in his arrival, as Annita had already delivered nine children before him—all in the very same bed where they had been conceived, in a room whose only furnishings were a rough beechwood chest and a crucifix nailed to the wall. In significance of his place in the family he was given the name Ultimo, or last; just as his

25

eldest brother was called Primo. In so naming him we can infer a desire, almost a plea to God, to end the procreation of the Gori spouses."

I hadn't been prepared to hear such a wealth of detail, but was transfixed by my elderly companion's measured, unhurried cadences and did not interrupt him.

"The Goris were one of the eighteen *mezzadri,* the sharecropping families who worked the lands owned by the Conti Terrosi—people whose entire existence was backbreaking labor in the rock-strewn fields of Chianti, whose ungenerous soil rewarded their attentions with modest crops that had to be divided with the *padrone,* the landowner. The Terrosi family received this payment in their splendid Castello Susi, where they had resided for six hundred years or more; though today, alas, it has become a vacation resort for the well-to-do."

The cemetery now behind us, he pressed down the accelerator and the old Alfa Romeo turned onto an unpaved road that craned slightly up a hill bordered by cypress trees, whose leaves caused the sunlight to dapple on the pebbled path before us.

"Gosto," the story continued, "known in the closest village as 'I Gori,' was stocky and short, illiterate and reserved, and possessed the strength of a *Chianina* bull. He was born on that same farm, as had his father, grandfather, great-grandfather and great-great-grandfather. 'We have always been here, our line unbroken,' he would boast, to which Annita, who was born in Cetona on the south side of Siena, would remind him, as if it made any difference, that his great-great-*great*-grandfather had lived for a while in an entirely separate *podere;* to which Gosto, with a shrug, would point out that this was still the property of the Terrosi, and within rifle-shot of Le Macie. So it was scarcely any different at all.

"By this time Gosto was completely bald, with a sunken face and fathomless eyes. He was extremely devoted to the Madonna and always wore a cord around his neck with a wooden crucifix he had himself carved from an olive branch. He worked from sunrise to sunset on the Terrosi acres along-side the other men from the sharecropping families. He spoke little but prayed constantly. He never missed a mass or even a vespers, and when the church bells echoed in the valleys announcing the canonical hours, he would go and chant his prayers at a shrine to the Virgin, strewing fresh flowers before her effigy, flowers he had gathered in the fields while working. Such shrines had been erected all over the Terrosi properties, and all of them were thickly laid with the dried petals of Gosto's offerings.

Annita was the sole child of her mother Virginia—a rarity in those days; certainly she made up for her mother's lack of fecundity. She dressed always in black as a mark of respect for her bereavements, but the black also served partly to disguise the way in which her body had been deformed by the delivery of ten children. Despite which, she was in many ways quite beautiful. She had long peppery hair that she gathered up in a bun, and which she let fall only before slipping beneath the bed sheets. Her face, while dry and hard, was sculpted and angular, not round like a bread loaf, as was the case with most of her neighboring wives, and her eyes were quick and bright; one could not look on her for long but to notice her unique appeal.

"On the whole, Annita had accepted her destiny; she loved her family and cared for the home as though it were a grand manor house. She seemed to spend most of her days on her knees, either scrubbing the terracotta floors with a wire brush, or clasping her sacred rosary beads in devotion as she prayed before the large crucifix Gosto had mounted on the bedroom wall. On Sundays, with the help of her mother, she would cook a lavish meal: *crostini* with chicken livers, egg *tagliatelle*, and a rabbit or pheasant roasted in the hearth. Her specialty was a honey, rosemary and walnut cake that she would bake for the local parish priest, Don Oraldo, and present to him each Sunday after mass."

Here the old *signore* was forced to halt his soliloquy for a moment to battle with the steering wheel, as the Alfa Romeo was having some difficulty on the steep country road. I waited in silence till he was ready to begin again.

"In those times the *mezzadri* were obliged to be self-sufficient, so Chianti was not then, as it is today, dominated by vines and olives. In fact the main crops were grains produced for flour, beets grown for sugar, mulberries to nourish the silkworms, canvas for textiles, and all sorts of fruits, legumes, and vegetables. But as even we who love it know, this is a harsh and rocky land"—here he lay his hand on my thigh for a moment to signify our mutual understanding—"and there seemed never to be enough.

"For this reason the population of Chianti was always sparse, and even today only a fifth of the land is cultivated, with the remainder yet woodland. But Nature is fair in all things: where she bestows scant quantities, she compensates with excellence. The *mezzadro* who may, given the choice, have preferred to satisfy his hunger with abundance, was fortunate in that the little he did have was of superb quality.

"Their homes were solid structures; surely you have seen them. They yet stand, though long abandoned. Nothing can bring them down. They were built with stones collected in the fields, some of them centuries old—in fact many were from the foundations of medieval castles or towers dating from the time when Chianti had been the theatre of the bloody, cruel, and seemingly endless clashes between the armies of Siena and Florence.

"Typically the homes were built on two floors, with the ground level incorporating the pens for the calves, the cages for the rabbits, and the barnyard. In front the chickens ran loose, while at the rear was the sty. The tang of excrement and mud would rise to the upper floor, where the family lived. One passed the threshold into a bare living room with a huge hearth, its few furnishings hewn out of raw wood—a table, a few lopsided chairs, and the inevitable kneading trough to store the flour and where the dough for the bread was made. From this area one could directly access the bedchambers, which were miserable unadorned quarters, its beds mere jute bags filled with straw and dry leaves resting on simple wooden planks. Often the rooms were linked to each other with no corridor, so that the concept of privacy was non-existent—a luxury possible only in the reveries of the well-to-do.

"The toilets were out of doors, more often than not a simple hole in into the ground and surmounted by a board. To wash up one went to the brook; and during winter the family members would take turns immersing themselves in tubs filled with water heated in voluminous cauldrons on the fireplace.

"In short, life was harsh in Chianti, not significantly different than it had been in the Middle Ages. The men were in charge of cultivating the fields, slaughtering the pigs, and making the salamis; the women's task was to look after the house and spin the wool. The children were assigned chores as soon as they could walk, and were taught to tend the farm animals, to accompany the sheep to the pastures, to look after the silkworms, and to fetch water daily from the creek, as what was pulled from the wells was often insalubrious.

"Schooling was for the wealthy, and recreation limited to a few religious feasts when the families would get together and dance in the barnyards of the various *poderi*. During winter they suffered terribly from cold and huddled desperately before the fireplace; the only light was supplied by oil lamps, as candles were considered a luxury. In practical terms the *mezzadri* possessed only the rags they wore, as everything else was the property of the landowner. It was a brutally hard life filled with sacrifice, made endurable only by the sure knowledge that a better existence awaited them in the next world—as long as they attended mass and lived in the spirit of the Lord."

He trailed off for a moment as we approached an ancient cemetery enclosed by a plastered wall. Here he parked and we exited the car, and once again he crooked his arm for me to take. Together we made our way toward the wrought-iron gate, which fell open before us at the slightest pressure, with only a few shrill creaks to protest our trespass. As soon as we had entered, the old man led me to the far end of the enclosure, past some freshly laid gravesites. Then he resumed speaking, in a kind of dreamy rush, as though he were in a kind of trance.

Chapter 5

Primo Gori

"The eldest child of Annita and Gosto, Primo, was born in 1888. His birth was cause for a grand celebration; a male heir, the *primo* to whom Gosto would pass on his store of early knowledge and wisdom. Also, it had been a problematic birth, so much so that Annita's life hung in the balance; she lost a great quantity of blood, and it is said that her screams could be heard resounding down the valleys all the way to the *podere Stella.*" As he named this farm, the *signore* pointed to a location vaguely eastwards. "But she survived, which added even more joy to the occasion.

"Alas, she was many weeks recovering and was obliged to remain in bed. Primo spent the first few months of his life cradled in the arms of his grandmother Virginia, the *nonna* of the house. She was in her early forties and had been widowed seven years earlier. Gino, Virginia's husband, had been hit by a calash that belonged to a wealthy aristocrat while returning from celebrations honouring twenty years of Italian unification. The cart didn't even stop and his body was found the following day by a wandering vagrant. The crime remained unsolved and unpunished and was in fact archived by the *Carabinieri* as an accident.

"Virginia now found solace in her loneliness in the form of her first grandchild. The only time she parted from him was when she took him from his cot to his mother's room to be breast-fed. Annita did her duty, but was so depleted by the effort that she could not but regard her infant with anything other than apathy. Perhaps for this reason, this early lack of a mother's love and attention, Primo's childhood was not a happy one.

"It was also marred by gossip. As the child grew, the malicious declared that he was the spitting image of Count Terrosi, the *padrone* of the *Macie,* whose custom it was to pay courtesy visits to the housewives during the hours the men were working the fields. Primo's hair, like the Count's, was thin and carrot-colored, and covered an equally low forehead. His frame was bony and his hands petite. He in no way resembled his bull-like father. Gosto himself never seemed, after the initial joy at his birth, to accept the boy as his successor—though less due to the rumors than to the weaknesses in his character. Primo had no spine for toil, no endurance, no strength of will. Eventually Gosto, with Annita's accord, decided to send him to the seminary, but the parish priest concluded that Primo lacked the adequate temperament for an ecclesiastical life, and turned him down.

"Primo seemed unable to forge a bond with anyone. His younger siblings never admired him as is usually the case with an older brother; in fact they virtually ignored him. He had no friends, no particular interests, and no real talents. In the mornings he would lug himself lazily to the fields, his head hung low and a wobble in his step, and pass the day mired in equal parts by indifference and ineptitude.

"At sunset, after supper, he didn't join the rest of his family in the customary gathering around the fireplace, but would lay himself down on his couch, facing the wall, and fall asleep, all but unmissed by the others. Only with his *nonna* Virginia did he remain connected, and she defended him from his father's rages, made excuses for his sloth and shirking, and stood between father and son to prevent the infliction of corporal punishment. When Virginia was not around, Primo resigned himself to his father's blows; he never shed tears, as if he were aware of being a chronic disappointment, deserving of his father's fists and his mother's disdain.

"His listlessness was invincible. Even after puberty, he showed no interest in the female sex. His parents tried to match him with a wife, but gave up because no girl would agree to have him; he gave none any reason to. He seemed destined to live his life in the bleakest isolation."

We now reached the far end of the cemetery and Primo's squalid burial site. The *signore* removed his hat, observed a moment of silence, then continued.

"The Terrosi were the first family in the area to purchase a steam-powered harvester, and on a scorching day in 1912 they held a celebration to inaugurate this prodigy of technology. Many adjoining landowners were invited; musicians played and wine flowed freely. Many of the guests' jaws dropped in disbelief when the demonstration of the harvester's operation commenced; the power and rapidity of the threshing was beyond what any of them had ever seen. The Terrosi beamed with pride, enjoying the envy of their noble neighbors.

"Leonardo, the foreman of both the *Macie* and the *Stella poderi,* was a domineering figure, much feared within the community. Noticing Primo idly dawdling during the demonstration, he ordered the young man to climb atop the harvester and help deposit the bundles of grain into the maw of the machine. Everything that followed seemed to occur in the blur of a moment: Primo clambered up but lost his balance, put his foot wrong, and rent the air with a shriek as he was pulled into the device. It digested him like a prehistoric beast, the cogs and spirals grinding him to bits; after a few seconds it spat out a tangled mass of gore flecked with wheat seeds and shreds of clothing. Only Primo's straw hat emerged somehow intact, an image of absurdity amidst the horror.

"Ultimo, who was four years old at the time, witnessed the entire event while holding the hand of his sister Giuseppina until she pulled herself from his grip by fainting.

"Primo had not yet reached his twenty-fifth birthday, and his funeral was very likely the only occasion in his life when tears were shed on his behalf. But even then the most malignant of tongues wagged that only a supremely idiotic *bischero* could have come to such an undignified end."

We stood now in contemplative silence before Primo's long-neglected tombstone. Eventually the *signore*, whose name I had yet to learn, replaced the Borsalino on his head and invited me to move a little further on.

Chapter 6

Delfino Gori

We now stood before a second tombstone. My mysterious companion released his grip on my arm and dolefully began a second narration.

"Delfino arrived two years after Primo and from the start he was all that Primo wasn't. His delivery was swift and pain-less, and as soon as he came to light he appeared healthy and chubby, with ruddy cheeks and a strong voice. As he grew he became increasingly jovial and warm-hearted; his was a lov-ing temperament and an acute intelligence. He never gave his parents a moments' worry. Because of Primo's deficiencies, Delfino was given premature responsibilities in the running of the farm, and he accepted them without resentment.

"As a toddler, he developed a passion for hunting and eager-ly sought from his father all the knowledge and training that Primo had spurned. He rigged ingenious traps for jackrabbits and pheasants, became proficient in digging out porcupines, and needed no net to catch thrushes, sparrows and swifts—all of which he would carry home in the leather bag his father had made for him. He loved good cooking and enjoyed presenting his *nonna* and his *mamma* with fresh game.

"He was also a practical joker. He amused himself by hid-ing toads and snakes in the pockets of his sisters' dresses, but despite these frequent japes they adored him.

"He mastered birdcalls, expertly twisting his tongue and lips and calibrating his breath to produce exactly the song of whatever breed he wished to imitate. For his eighth birthday a passing wayfarer, enchanted by his warbling, gave him the harmonica that became his most precious possession. During breaks in the vineyards and fields he would pluck it from his shirt pocket and refresh the workers with sweet melodies. He learned popular tunes but also improvised his own, and during the winter would fill the house with music to pass the long evening vigils around the crackling hearth, delighting the entire family except for Primo, who was always already asleep.

"Delfino wasn't handsome; he had the animal strength of his father, but was shorter and stockier. Yet his acorn-colored hair fell over his large forehead in a way that made him look agreeable and jaunty, and his maroon eyes had a mocking glint; and his smile, despite his crooked, opaque teeth, was irresistible. He was a hard and enthusiastic worker and despite not knowing any other way of life, seemed to embrace this one so fully that he might have chosen it from a dozen alternatives. He thrived on the sweat and the fatigue, the endless days enduring either sizzling summer sun or blistering winter wind.

"In due course he became engaged to Lucia, a radiantly lovely girl, the daughter of the owner of the nearby Combi flour mill. But then the Great War broke out and Delfino was summoned to serve his country, fighting to defend the northeast of Italy against an Austrian invasion. The wedding date was set for his homecoming; but Delfino never came home. On the twenty-second of October in the year 1917, the Italian infantry under the command of General Cadorna was wiped out at Caporetto—first by a tempest of artillery fire, then by a barrage of toxic gasses, and finally in a bloody man-to-man bayonet massacre within the chilly trenches. Italy's losses at Caporetto included nearly twelve thousand dead, nineteen thousand wounded, three hundred thousand prisoners, four thousand deserters, thirty-two hundred cannons, sixteen hundred bombards, three thousand machineguns, and three thousand rifles.

"The news of Delfino's death was delivered by the parish priest, Don Oraldo, exactly two months and three days after the battle. He also returned the boy's beloved harmonica, on which was scratched in a scarcely legible manner the words *Lucia & Delfino.*

"And here, young man, is his grave." The *signore* sighed and once again removed his hat. "The family fell into a state of depression at the news that their golden son would never return. Both Gosto and Annita seemed to age twenty years overnight, and their shoulders stooped thenceforth. They were dispirited and crestfallen.

"On the day Delfino fell, Ultimo was but nine."

Chapter 7

Maria Pia Gori

The aged *signore* swiveled his head in my direction, surprising me by for the first time by saying my name.

"Dario, to go to your maker at so tender an age, or even at birth, was no remarkable thing; indeed it was part of the routine of life at that time, and each and every family shouldered their shared of untimely bereavements. The Goris were no exception. Infants died as a result of a number of calamities. In Chianti malnutrition was not a problem, as it was in the cities; but poor hygiene and infections were chronic. One was forced to live in close proximity with animals and their effluvia, especially in winters, and vaccines were only available to the rich. Country folk resorted to homemade remedies, such as compresses of herbs and folk brews that were essentially useless. It was nearly impossible to get a doctor to call, as they were reluctant to travel over miles of jerky roads in an ungainly cart to visit peasant families who were only able to pay them in eggs and salamis.

"Maria Pia arrived in 1892, the first girl of the Gori family. It was a great joy of course for Annita, but even Gosto relished the novelty of registering a female birth at the church. At the time of the delivery Gosto had been picking olives; when the news was shouted up to him he leapt from the tree like a feline. Leonardo the foreman did not permit him to go home before the end of his shift, but gave him a short break in which he could visit the closest shrine to the Madonna and recite a prayer of thanksgiving. He knelt before the small altar he had erected and shed grateful tears.

"The baby girl was to all appearances healthy; she was animated and alert and took her milk with avidity. But this idyll did not long continue. After a few weeks, she descended into pyrexias. She stopped feeding, no longer able to take milk through her inflamed throat. Annita strove to do all in her power to make the infant suckle, but in vain: the child's life dwindled to an end, marked by the screams of grief of her *nonna* Virginia.

"Gosto had never even touched his daughter; his heavy, blunt fingers were larger than her tiny limbs, and he had been fearful of hurting her. The first and last time he held her was when he placed her into her minuscule coffin. The family had no certain idea of what had happened to Maria Pia, but it seems clear she had contracted diphtheria, a disease that was bitterly common and very often fatal.

"They interred the child, her casket covered with holy images, just two months after her birth. And within a few weeks, the Goris, like most families of the time, ended their mourning and resumed their humble life. Death was common, but grief was a luxury. Even so, they marked the depth of their loss by never again mentioning Maria Pia's name. It became one of many forgotten names in innumerable Chianti cemeteries who share the same sad fate, that the year of their births had been the year of the deaths."

We stood in silence before the small grave, its tombstone obscured by a crust of dried moss. The *signore* gripped my arm again, which by now I knew meant he wished to walk. As we moved away, he picked up his narrative.

Chapter 8

Tosca Gori - Antonia Gori

"Maria Pia's loss was lessened by the arrival in 1894 of Tosca, who managed to endure an exceptionally frigid winter made worse by scant food. The crops had been greatly damaged by a succession of shattering hailstorms, so that the harvest was greatly reduced; and Count Terrosi, inflexible even in the face of adversity, was resolute in demanding his fifty per cent share of the yield, leaving the Goris and the other families running his *poderi* on the brink of starvation.

"Yet despite having been born in so unlucky a season, Tosca thrived. Despite her diminutive size she was tough and resilient and appeared to sail through the harsh conditions as if they were a summer idyll. She was a graceful child, with a dark complexion dappled with freckles and jet-black hair like her *nonna* Virginia's. She was also quite lively, and the first word out of her mouth was, tellingly, not *mamma* but *Delfino*, the name of her adored older brother.

"Unfortunately, destiny can be perverse; and after surviving such lean times, Tosca at sixteen months was struck down by a fulminating bronchopneumonia, just when life was getting easier for the family. This bereavement was even harder for the family than Maria Pia's, because unlike her sister, Tosca had lived long enough to develop an indelible character: radiant, joyful, and courageous. Everything about her argued against so early a departure from the world; but such was the tenor of life in Chianti. Death arrived without warning and granted no distinctions. Despite the ache of their grief, the Goris remained devout believers and fervently continued practising their religion. Gosto in particular never missed daily vespers and the family attended mass together every Sunday as well as every holy day of obligation.

"When Tosca perished, Annita was again expecting; and two months after her daughter's funeral she delivered Antonia, the third consecutive Gori female. Uncannily, she was the very image of Tosca; she might have been a long-delayed twin. Antonia also repeated the ease with which Tosca had been weaned, and became as obsessively fond of Delfino, who by this time was five years of age, and who returned the adoration. As soon as he acquired sufficient strength, he would lift her from her cot and carry her to his own bed to cuddle.

"As a toddler Antonia discovered that the burnt stubs of charcoal in the fireplace left marks when rubbed against the walls; and so she began to express herself with a series of elaborate doodles and squiggles. Initially she was scolded, but as soon as her mother took the charcoal from her she would break into sobs, shedding tears like a fountain. Eventually it was settled that Antonia was permitted to draw on the walls within the fireplace itself, and she happily agreed to this condition.

"During the course of an Easter blessing, Don Oraldo, who possessed a predilection for art in any form, found his attention drawn to these abstract designs, he convinced a renowned painter in Siena to make her a gift of a paper album and some colored pencils. Delighted, Antonia devoted all her spare time to drawing, and taught herself to sketch landscapes and portraits of notable craftsmanship for a girl her age.

"But somewhere it was written that the Gori daughters should never enjoy long life, and at the age of thirteen, just when the woman she would become was emerging from the girl she had been, Antonia contracted smallpox—a disease of distressing commonness in those days. Unlike the sisters who predeceased her, Antonia was aware of her eventual fate and focused all her agonies into a series of bleakly lugubrious abstract drawings.

"At her funeral were present not only her brothers Primo and Delfino, but the other siblings whose births had followed hers in the succeeding thirteen years: Tancredi, Ricciotti, Giuseppina, and Carlotta."

Chapter 9

*Tancredi Gor*i

We passed the three adjacent tombstones, but I had no time to contemplate the unlucky fates of the trio of sisters, as the *signore* tugged me towards yet another gravesite—this one etched with the name Tancredi Gori.

"Tancredi was born in 1899 and was something of a blend of Primo and Delfino. A valorous boy, he was physically powerful, but possessed no outstanding talents or skills. He was quiet and bashful, but was a hard and tireless worker. Almost as soon as he learned to walk, he was put in charge of the chickens and rabbits; his only failing in the dispatch of these duties was that he grew far too fond of the creatures, and when his mother made plans to slaughter and cook one of them, he invariably attempted to hide it from her—then later refused utterly to eat it.

"Don Oraldo was captivated by the little boy's sensibility, and when Tancredi reached the age of ten the priest came to speak to Gosto about sending him to the seminary. Such an opportunity was considered a great honor, for priests were held in high esteem; and as a seminarian, Tancredi would undertake studies that would vastly improve his understanding, his abilities, and his material wealth.

"But as it happened the boy was listening behind the door, and when he realized that the priest was encouraging his father to send him away, he broke into sobs and ran into the room, imploring his *babbo* not to make him go. Gosto was moved by his son's emotion and, turning to Don Oraldo, replied simply, *'No, grazie Padre.'* The cleric took this as a personal affront; he pivoted on his heels, grabbed his country-priest Saturn hat, hiked up the hem of his long black cassock, and departed the *podere* in a rage.

"Tancredi was ever grateful to his father for not having forced him into the seminary. He was acutely aware that if he hadn't requested otherwise, his *babbo* would have been only to happy to agree to the plan, thus bringing honor on the family by having a priest as a son. But he had set aside his personal ambitions for the desperate wishes of his child. Because of this, Tancredi loved Gosto more than any of the other children. His affection for his mother, by contrast, while sincere, was more a matter of duty. He was never in conflict with her, but neither was there ever any tangible public manifestation of their bond. Their relationship was, in a word, cordial.

"Tancredi was eighteen when Delfino was killed in 1917. In Italy the war had degenerated into a bloody killing spree. To stem the slaughter, the state was forced to enlist the youths born in 1899. Consequently Tancredi was called to duty at a time when the family was still unaware of Delfino's fate.

"After an accelerated training in Florence, Tancredi was sent to the front lines, where he fought with honor on the Piave in what turned out to be the great resurgence of the Italian army. Italy won the day at Vittorio Veneto, but Tancredi lost his life there; and the medals and honors that were delivered to the devastated Gori family did nothing to ease their howling grief.

"On the monument erected in the village commemorating the local youths killed during the first World War, Gori is the only name engraved twice: a price far too high for a family already reeling from so many untimely losses. For the remainder of his days, Gosto blamed himself for having succumbed to Tancredi's youthful tears. Had he been a sterner father and sent his son to the seminary, he would not have been taken from him so cruelly. He interpreted it as divine punishment."

Chapter 10

Ricciotti Gori

Another several steps brought us to the resting place of Ricciotti, the sixth Gori son.

"Ricciotti," the old man confided, "was born cerulean as wax in 1902, and in absolute silence; he was both deaf and mute and, even worse, without the use of his lower limbs. Don Oraldo, on first seeing this bent, incomplete attempt at humanity, was certain the infant could survive no more than a few hours, and so both baptized him and granted him extreme unction on the day he came into the world.

"But the child astounded all by living on despite his afflictions—and also by the joyful, even mirthful character he possessed. Ricciotti turned out to be a remarkable child: ever serene and happy, it seemed that his terrible burdens lightened rather than oppressed him. He was adored by his mother and siblings, and Gosto was rarely separated from him. In the morning he would lift him from his bed, bathe him gently in a tub before the fireplace, and dry and dress him before consigning him to Annita, who would serve him a breakfast of ersatz chicory coffee and bread dipped in wine with a generous sprinkling of sugar. Ricciotti would thank them in the only way he knew how: by shining his luminescent eyes at them.

"Gosto would then prop the lad on his shoulders as though he were a sack of clothes and carry him to the fields, where he would settle him comfortably beneath a tree. When Gosto had finished tying or pruning a row, he would move Ricciotti with him to the next strip he was about to tackle. Ricciotti one day took up two apples that had fallen from the tree in whose shade his father had placed him, and soon learned what fun it was to throw them in the air and catch them. With the passage of a few months he was able to juggle three, then four, then five at the same time.

"During the village feasts he turned this ability into a kind of attraction, and Annita knit him a jester's outfit with little bronze bells that dangled and jangled from different corners. The local rumor was that these were chimes once used for religious services, donated by the parish priest to support Ricciotti's endeavor.

"Soon Ricciotti's juggling made him the most well-known of the Gori clan, so much so that he was able to begin charging for his services and was hired to entertain wealthy families at their private parties. Gosto and Delfino would take turns carrying him on their back to the Saturday markets, going from village to village, covering scores of miles on foot. During these endless walks, Delfino played his harmonica and Ricciotti, on his shoulders, would place his bony hand on his brother's Adam's apple so as to "hear" the music through the vibrations; and with his other hand he would wave in time to the tune. Seeing them thus was altogether engaging; they seemed to have some kind of symbiotic relationship, as sometimes happens among very differing species in the natural world.

"Thus Ricciotti, as improbable as it may seem, because the sole member of the Gori family capable of creating his own job outside the farm and bringing home real earnings. They considered this soundless, smiling son a true gift from God.

"At the end of the war there was an outbreak of the dreaded Spanish influenza; this became known as the Great Flu, and it did not spare Chianti as it raged across the world, killing some fifteen million people: including Ricciotti. For the first time, Gosto's religious faith wavered; he paid fewer visits to the shrines, and even began skipping mass on Sundays. He took to drinking, and soon became a chronic alcoholic, bitter and blaspheming. The now elderly Don Oraldo failed to comfort him, nor could Leonardo or even Count Terrosi restore him to peace of mind.

"Annita, in contrast, revealed her iron spine after Ricciotti's death. It seemed that each and every blow only succeeded in strengthening her will. Not only did she remain steadfast in her faith, she added her aged mother to those whose care she must daily attend, and she did so lovingly, without complaint.

"Gosto seemed fated to die from abuse of grappa; but in fact he went on a Sunday in 1929, collapsing suddenly after he stood up from the table after one of his wife's succulent meals. In that oddly chosen moment, his grief-stricken heart simply stopped beating. I believe he was exhausted, worn out by life. Ultimo at the time was twenty-one.

"Annita would not follow him till much later, and not till six years after having buried that 'secular tree' her mother Virginia had become."

Chapter 11

Giuseppina Gori

My companion averted his gaze from Ricciotti's grave and indicated Gosto's, a few plots away from that of his beloved son. He then turned to me and for a searing moment our eyes locked; I could feel his eagerness to fill in the missing pieces of the family story he was telling me so avidly—like water from a jug, trying to pour through too narrow a spot.

"Giuseppina was born seven years and two months after Ricciotti—another chance for Annita to have the daughter she so desired, and Virginia the granddaughter. It was immediately evident that this child possessed something special; a twining of humility and heart, and an innate appetite for life.

"Mercifully, her childhood was uneventful; but in her teens she went through a transformation that astonished the entire province. From a gangly, loose-limbed girl she became, seemingly overnight, an extraordinarily beautiful woman, as enchanting as the most luminous star in the heavens. At sixteen, she was the most eagerly sought female in all of southern Chianti. Tall as a sapling cypress, as exquisitely rounded as the surrounding hills, her hair fell about her shoulders like spills of the blackest ink. She looked, in fact, uncannily like a portrait of an Etruscan woman in a fresco then recently discovered in an archaeological site close to the village—and thus her nickname, *Pina l'Etrusca*.

"Giuseppina was the quintessence of femininity. It didn't matter that she dressed in drab peasant clothing; her regal bearing shone through. During mass, she drew more worshipful looks than the statue of the Madonna. She was the oneiric vision, as well as the erotic dream of each and every single male in the area. But she was indifferent to such attentions; her simple heart was completely given over to *mamma, babbo, nonna,* and her siblings.

"Pina spent her days at the creek, plunging her smooth hands into the Serchia's icy currents, washing not only the Goris' clothes, but those of neighboring families, a service she performed in exchange for some modest provisions. To pass the time while laundering she would sing. Possessed of a paradisiacal voice, she crooned local folk songs or improvised tunes of her own making. It was said that that when the water got colder, her voice became high pitched.

"Pina was the daughter everyone would have chosen for themselves; the sister too. She would become a very important figure in the life of Ultimo."

We had now retraced our steps to the gate of the cemetery; yet he had shown me no gravesite for Giuseppina. So it was only natural that I asked whether this paragon of womanhood still lived. He turned toward my slyly, then put his finger to his lips to signal that I must be patient.

Chapter 12

Carlotta Gori

Back in the Alfa Romeo Guilia, the old man extracted a cigar from a small tin box and lit it before starting the engine. He smoked it with gusto as he drove back to the village, sometimes taking such lengthy puffs that one might think he was inhaling the breath of life itself. When the cigar had sufficiently restored him, he picked up the thread of his story.

"The ninth fruit of the marriage of Annita and Gosto was very different from all the others. In the terminology of our present day, we would call her autistic. Carlotta seemed at all times to be living in a kind of parallel world. She was very different from the darkly beautiful Pina; she was blonde with green eyes, which gave her an otherworldly look that suited her character.

"When Ultimo drove the sheep to pasture she accompanied him—or perhaps 'followed' is a better word, for she trailed some yards behind him, prancing and twirling like a ballerina, occasionally pausing to collect wildflowers which she would later weave into her hair. She was far more in tune with nature than with other people; hares and pheasants felt no alarm at her presence, indeed they often approached her. It wasn't at all unusual to see her being escorted by a swarm of bees or even horseflies, which she allowed to alight on her pale skin, though no insects, not even ravenous mosquitoes, ever dared to pierce her flesh.

"She was captivated by scents and odors, and would drink in the seasonal perfumes of Chianti till she seemed to be giving them off herself. So deeply was this strange little girl in tune with her surroundings that she could sense an approaching storm long before any cloud appeared. She would raise her eyes and point to the sky, and excitedly mumble incoherent phrases. Hours later, a deluge would commence, as if summoned.

"Despite all this, she scarcely ever smiled, and had a melancholy aura that was reflected by a hollowness in her eyes and an emptiness in her expression. Only at three years of age did she walk, and at four spoke her first word, which was 'bee,' which came forth in a moment of intense excitement, as if it were the answer to a riddle she alone had been posed. During the winter months, when the outdoors were less accessible to her, she would seem to shut down, rocking endlessly on her bed as if comforting herself, and repeating the words, 'bees, bees, honey, sweet honey.'

"And yet she was beautiful in her own way, Dario; can you understand that? Strange and frightening and beautiful, like a celestial spirit; an angel lost on earth."

He fell silent after delivering this judgment. We returned to the village bar; the sun had now set and a wind had kicked up, sweeping the fallen leaves from the lime trees across the narrow square. We sat for a moment in stillness; then he opened the mahogany door of his glove box and withdrew a maroon envelope, and placed it in my lap.

Chapter 13

The envelope

"Dario," said the old *signore* in very solemn tones, "divine providence guided you to me."

This was a surprising pronouncement to hear from someone I had met only a few hours before. And yet I was perfectly at ease in this venerable man's company. I even felt I was beginning to know him; there was a hint of distress in his otherwise avid relation of the Gosti family story; recalling these events seemed to cause him pain, as though it was more confession than narration.

"I ask only this of you," he said; "return to *podere Macie* sometime in the next few days and deliver this envelope. It was my intention to do so myself, but..." He sighed and looked wistful for a moment; then turned to me and smiled. "As I said: providence has given me you, instead."

I took the envelope from him. "All right. But I think I ought at least to know your name."

He seemed about to tell me; then thought twice, and closed his lips. A moment later he said, "Once Ultimo has opened the packet, let him tell you my name. If he so wishes."

This was so strange an answer that I felt compelled to ask, "Why? What is Ultimo to you?"

He chuckled, and said, "What, indeed?" He stared at the glass of his windshield for a few moments, as if in search of an appropriate response. At last he turned to me and said with sudden earnestness, "What is Ultimo, you ask? Ultimo is Chianti!"

This remarkable assertion hung in the air between us for a

moment; then all the fire went out of him and he was once again a feeble old man. "I've got to go now, Dario," he said. "It's been many years since last I was here, but I have no regrets at having put off my errand this long, for now I see that this is how it was meant to be. Now, the responsibility is yours. *Addio,* my young friend; I'm afraid our paths will not cross again, not even by chance, as tomorrow I return to my country."

This was all so strange and dramatic that I found myself unable to think of what question I ought to say next. Instead I found myself getting out of his car and waving to him in a kind of daze as he drove off, raising a slight cloud of dust. I watched till he vanished over the horizon, at which point all I could do was get back on my Vespa and take myself home.

I found my mother working before the crackling fireplace. I handed her the *porcini* mushrooms, which she accepted with delight and instantly sautéed in olive oil with garlic and parsley just as Ultimo had suggested. Later, as I sat with my parents at the table, my father asked what I had been up to all day.

"Niente," I said.

"Really? Nothing at all?"

I shrugged, as all teenagers do before parental inquisition. After dinner I went immediately to bed, as I had a tough shift at the winery next day. As I lay on my back, my neck resting on my palms, I reflected with bewilderment on my encounters with the two old men. All I'd planned to do that morning was hunt for mushrooms; I'd ended up being drawn into the middle of a curious relationship whose roots apparently went back generations. How could I ever explain such a thing to my father? I could barely comprehend it myself. I had no idea what might be the link between sclerotic old Ultimo and the elegant *signore;* and my efforts to guess had the effect of hot chamomile tea. I was soon in slumber, cradled in the arms of Morpheus.

Chapter 14

The Visit

Remembering all this now, so many years later, as I hurried to Ultimo's farmhouse in response to the summons on my answering machine, I realized I had only a vague recollection of what the elegant *signore* looked like. As he foretold, we were never again to meet; and my teenage eyes were not yet so expert in the reading of human faces, as to register anything from his but the impression of ripe old age.

Once I reached the *Macie* I parked the car near Ultimo's tool shed, then sprang up the steps to the chestnut-sheltered porch before the entry. The door was ajar and swung wide at my touch, opening onto the living room.

The first thing that caught my eye was a young woman seated on the sofa before the hearth. My unexpected appearance gave her a jolt, and she leapt to her feet; then she recovered and approached me with a welcoming look in her green, almond eyes. She was a handsome woman, somewhere in her thirties, of medium stature, slender and well built, her olive skin glowing in the firelight. Her long, silken hair swayed as she walked, and her loose-fitting lace blouse billowed above her tight black skirt.

She grasped my hand firmly with long fingers devoid of adornment. I returned her grip slightly longer than was strictly necessary, as the warmth and smoothness of her palm was very pleasant.

"Dario?" she said, in a local cadence but with a slight accent that I couldn't place.

"Piacere," I said in a reserved manner, as she had—perhaps due to distraction—not yet offered her name.

"Ultimo isn't well; it's his heart. He had an episode three days ago but insisted on remaining here at the *Macie.* You know him, so I'm sure you understand; if he doesn't will it, a team of horses couldn't drag him to hospital. And anyway, at his age, a man should be allowed to decide his own fate. I don't know how long he has left. But he's perfectly lucid, and has been asking to see you."

It was the first I'd heard of any "episode," but I decided not to plague her with questions and instead merely asked to be taken to him.

She led me across the short length of the house, saying, "He's very weak, please don't fatigue him." I still couldn't identify her accent. Then, her eyes beginning to swell with tears, she left me at the door to Ultimo's room. I entered.

It was exactly as I recalled it: a simple brass bed, a chest, and a beech wood wardrobe with two cases propped atop it, covered with labels publicizing old travel agencies. Flanking the bed were a pair of nightstands he had inherited from his parents, of equal height but carved with different representations of mythological scenes. On one, a copper lantern with a bright pink shade was burning low. Ultimo lay on his back, immobile and gaunt; he looked indeed like a dying man. His eyes were shut but the lids seemed almost transparent, as though he were staring through them at the oak beams that crossed the ceiling.

I took the sole chair—the seat woven of straw, the legs uneven—and sat adjacent to him, at the head of the bead. His breathing was labored; he inhaled briskly through his nose, and exhaled with more difficulty through his lips. I leaned over and kissed his cold forehead, and stroked his silvery, still-thick hair. Beneath the pressure of my hand his skull felt frail, like those of the sparrows that local restaurants used to roast on spits, a local specialty now long banned.

Suddenly he came alive; he lashed out with his bony wrist and grasped my biceps. Such vitality from a man in his extremity alarmed me. Then his lids sprang open and he fixed his eyes on me, and the turquoise of his irises seemed to deepen as he recognized me.

"Dario, it's you?"

"So it is, Ultimo. I'm here."

He released his grip. "I need a spot of medicine." He jerked his thumb towards the nightstand.

I looked to where he had pointed, but saw no jar of pills; just a flask half-filled with wine and a packet of unfiltered *nazionale* cigarettes, the ones so strong a single puff can generate a tumor.

I hesitated only a moment. "Which one do you want, Ultimo?"

"The medicine!" he said testily, as though I were being stupid. "Pour me a glass from the fiasco." Then he thought a moment and added, "You may as well light me a cigarette too."

I had never contradicted Ultimo; yet I was aware that I was about to do the most stupid thing possible. All the same, I poured him a glass and handed it to him; he gripped it with scrawny, trembling fingers. Then I tapped out a cigarette, lit it, and placed it between his lips, as though he were a dying soldier in some old black-and-white movie. With difficulty he propped himself up and sucked mightily, expelling the smoke with a little glottal burst as he had always done, ever since I had met him.

"So, *nini,*" he said, using the term seniors always applied to the young, despite my now being well into my forties. "How's life?"

He appeared genuinely interested and quite alert, so I told him that all was well. Then I was sufficiently emboldened to ask the same of him, though it had never been my practice to ask him anything of a personal nature.

He shrugged, as if to say, you can see how it is with me. Then he took another puff from the cigarette and said, "I suppose I've reached the end of the road." He tipped the ashes onto the floor, then his expression darkened and he added, "I seem to be getting weaker. So I thought I might ask you to do one final thing for me."

"Of course, Ultimo. Anything."

"Tomorrow, if you can, go to the barn." He reached over to the bedstand drawer and pulled from it the very same coffee-colored envelope I had given him a quarter-century earlier. "You'll find the key in here, along with the document you delivered to me so long ago. You may now read it, but do so only when the circumstances are suitable."

I took the envelope from him but he kept his arm extended; I realized he wished me to shake his hand—he was ending our interview. I gripped his palm, which was cool and dry, like paper, and wrapped my fingers around his. I felt that we were sharing a moment of some great import. "I'll go at once," I said. "Tomorrow. I give you my word."

He seemed about to reply, but at that moment the young woman stepped into the room. I plucked the cigarette from his mouth as quickly and nonchalantly as I could, but there was no hiding the haze of bluish-grey smoke above his bed. She flew into an immediate rage.

"Are you out of your mind?" she barked in disgust, lunging forward and waving the smoke away from Ultimo. "Smoking in the presence of a dying man?" She glanced down at my feet. "Ashes on the floor! Filthy! Get out of here!"

I was glad that I'd spared Ultimo her fury by shifting the

blame to myself; but I was truly upset at having distressed her at all, especially because I'd hoped to exchange a few words with her afterwards, and possibly get to know her better. Strangely, her flash of anger only rendered her more attractive in my eyes.

Ultimo grinned in delight at our connivance as I headed to the door. I took care to keep more than an arm's length from the young woman, lest she lash out and strike me. Once out of the room I scurried back to my car, well aware that I had taken on another burden from Ultimo, and that I might expect some unusual and difficult days ahead.

Chapter 15

9th October 2008

I had no idea how long I'd be gone, so first thing in the morning I set up an automated response for my email account. The book I had promised to complete could wait a few days; my agent would be in an uproar, but since she was on the other side of the world, all she could do was upbraid me electronically.

I stuffed my knapsack with what I supposed would be sufficient provisions, then slung it over my back, turned off the lights, locked my front door, and took a deep breath. Then I set off.

The air was unusually nippy for the time of year, and grew more so as I descended to the bottom of the valley. I was alone, and aware that I would likely have no company of any kind of the next several days; but many of us in Chianti are accustomed to solitude, and even welcome it as a respite from the frenetic rhythms of modern life. I had lived alone for many years now, with no wife beside me or even a woman friend to make claims on my time; in fact I survived very well without society of any kind, save for those infrequent times I paid a visit to my Contrada headquarters, where there was always a plethora of friendly faces. In this I was fulfilled; in fact I considered myself privileged.

The sun was splendid, climbing steadily into a pale blue sky empty but for the merest trace of cloud. As it rose it dispelled the hardest edge of the chill. I trod on, through a well-tended olive grove and around a very old vine that was in need of a drastic pruning. A pheasant suddenly bolted from a broom bush, screeching as it hopped away from me, higher each time till it eventually, rather clumsily, took flight. Once in the air it became the picture of grace; it gently altered its trajectory and disappeared into the distance, behind the upper scrim of a chestnut forest.

The path wove downward between a triumph of arbutus bushes and junipers, before snaking into an oak wood whose trees had now almost entirely shed their cloak of leaves. At the bottom of the valley, the air suddenly became quite humid, as I was nearing the Serchia, which yet awaited the abundant fall rainfalls that would transform it from a stream into a torrent. Fortunately for me, in its present shallow state it was easy to wade across.

Past the opposite bank, the country road began again to ascend. The ankles of my jeans had been wet through by the river; now the thighs soaked through as well, from brushing against clumps of dewy ferns. I felt curiously light-hearted; and then actually joyful, as I found a precious *cucco* mushroom, so near the path it seemed to be waiting just for me. I placed it in my pouch next to the arbutus fruits I'd picked early that day.

While I was tackling the sharp rise, I saw a golden oriole flutter through the branches, and the sight of its dazzling ochre plumage cast me back to the day I met Ultimo for the second time.

Chapter 16

28th October 1983

Two uneventful days had passed since I'd met the mysterious gentleman clad in the double-breasted jacket, Borsalino hat and suede gloves. The envelope he'd given me remained sealed, though I frequently handled it, examining its seams and surmising its weight as if by those means I could discern its contents.

Thursday of that week was a local religious holiday and since the winery was closed, I had the opportunity to discharge my commission and deliver the envelope to Ultimo Gori. This time, when I reached the *Macie,* I was careful to leave my Vespa on the trestle rather than lean it against the shed; in no way did I wish to irk Ultimo again. I might find my Vespa on his roof.

I then went to his vegetable garden, where I had found him before; but it was empty. Realizing he must be indoors, I climbed the flight of stone steps to his front door, then summoned my courage and knocked. Seconds later, he responded.

He seemed smaller than I recalled from our earlier meeting; more like an academic than a farmer. Perhaps it was the effect of the minuscule reading glasses perched on the tip of his nose. Certainly he was dressed in the same style, though in place of his woollen vest he now sported a green checked shirt; and once again, only one of the sleeves was buttoned at the wrist. I found myself tongue-tied before him, and while I searched for something to say he recognized me and took the initiative.

"Go away, you can't stay here!" he exclaimed, slamming the door in my face as if I were in the habit of harassing him. This rude treatment startled me, and snapped me out of my awkwardness. I certainly wasn't going to give in so easily. I propped the envelope against the outer wall of the house and pounded on the door with both fists.

"Go *away,*" he called through the door. "You can't stay here!"

"I heard you the first time," I said. "Is that all you can say? I know parrots with more conversation."

"Get your scrawny ass off my property! There, you prefer that?" Then, silence.

I got the distinct impression that he was lingering behind the door, waiting to see what I would do next. I almost turned away in disgust, but decided on one last gambit—which might not gain me entry, but would certainly surprise him.

"Primo, Giuseppina, Carlotta," I began reciting in ringing tones. "Tosca, Ricciotti, Maria Pia, Delf—" I broke off as the door swung open and he grabbed the collar of my shirt. His eyes were as cold as marble, and bored into mine with fury.

"Where did you come by those names?" he said. "What do you want from me?"

I gestured for him to release me, and he flung me into the house like a sack of grain. I smoothed my shirt front as he glared at me, his ribcage contracting like an accordion. Suddenly his eyes assumed an unexpected look of wariness. He swept back his thick hair, revealing a wrinkled forehead, and in this new state of fragile calm, he produced from the dresser two glasses and filled them both with red wine, handing one of them to me. He immediately drained his, filled it a second time, then rifled his breast pocket for a pack of unfiltered *nazionali*, placing one cigarette between his teeth. He struck a match on the rough surface of the fireplace tiles and lit it. All the while he watched me. Curiously this composure provoked in me more fear than did his earlier outburst.

I tried not to show my trepidation, and realized it would be up to me to break the ice. My eyes suddenly fell on a small, framed picture of a Chianti landscape. "Is that," I asked, "perhaps a drawing by your sister, Antonia?" Then I spotted another containing military medals tied with ribbons the color of the Italian flag. "And might these be the honors awarded your brother Tancredi?"

He narrowed one eye and observed me for what seemed like a long time. Then he opened a drawer and produced a small wooden harmonica. "I suppose," he said, "you can also guess to whom *this* belonged."

"Your brother Delfino," I said without hesitation.

He replaced the harmonica, then refilled his glass, took a long drag off his cigarette, and after releasing a stream of blue smoke in my direction, said, "Speak."

And so I told him of my encounter with the mysterious *signore* several days prior, taking care to omit no detail, however insignificant it might seem to me. He listened attentively, sitting backwards in his chair, arms crossed over its back, cigarette hanging from his lips. He offered not a single interruption, and when I concluded I handed him the envelope.

He turned it over in his calloused hands just as I had done, without opening it. A fly landed on the rim of his wineglass and he waved it away without removing his eyes from the envelope. Then he took the glass and downed its last gulp, as though to strengthen his resolve. He tore open the flap and removed a sheaf of folded pages, which he placed on the table, face down, without reading them. Then he turned the envelope upside down, and a key slipped from its interior into his waiting palm. He looked at it without expression, then rose to his feet, walked across the room, opened a tall oblong cabinet, and produced a rifle. He ran his hand gently over the barrel a few times, then deftly loaded it with buckshot, of the kind used for hunting wild boars.

And then he turned to me and said, "Take me to that son of a bitch."

"*Signor* Ultimo," I said, more terrified than ever by the cool malevolence he was displaying; "he's gone. He left the country for good the morning after I met him. He didn't tell me where; he never even told me his name. Please, put down the gun." A note of panic slipped into my last words.

To my surprise, he did as I asked, replacing the rifle on the rack in the cabinet. Then he went to the window and contemplated the Chianti hills in silence. I waited patiently until he pivoted on his heels and, to my surprise, said, "What is it, *nini*, that you aspire to do in life?"

The question was so sincere and his manner so cordial, that I was taken aback; but coming so soon after having him toss me over his threshold, his use of the affectionate term *nini* astonished me most of all. I could never have dreamed, at that moment, that he was to refer to me by that appellative for many years to come. But I did feel a bond forge between us, and my fears relaxed into the first blush of friendship.

I considered his question for a moment, then shrugged and admitted, "I don't know what it is I want, exactly."

He placed his hand on my shoulder and guided me into a room in which stood an ancient mirror. "Fix your gaze," he said, standing me before it; "contemplate and reflect upon yourself, on who you are."

I did as I was told with a little laugh of embarrassment. A few minutes later he motioned me to accompany him to the window.

"You love this territory, that's easy to see. You should share the history of these lands with those who deserve it; and you must do so without hesitation." He allowed for a slight dramatic pause, then pronounced: "You shall become a Chianti tour guide as you have always desired." He pronounced Chianti as the locals do, aspirating the 'c'.

That *was* exactly what I had always wanted, I now realized. How many times had I imagined leading such a life, and how was it possible for this strange old man to see into my hidden yearnings?

He opened another door and led me through it; now I was in a room crammed to the brim with an amazing bounty of books, geographical maps, documents, ancient scrolls, texts and manuscripts that seemed to have the Chianti territory as their common subject, and many of which appeared extremely rare. They seemed to be piled carelessly on top of one another in a riot of confusion, but I sensed that Ultimo had his own sense of order and knew exactly the location of every item. My eye was caught by the Repetti's geographical and historical dictionary, the *Dizionario Geografico Fisico Storico della Toscana*, as well as numerous ancient biographies of notable personages who had lived among these hills. I was assailed by a comforting aroma of antique paper and leather covers, and the light from the window was saturated with the exhalation of dust that had been deposited on the shelves and scaffolds over the course of many years.

"Nini," Ultimo said while clasping a leather-bound tome, "this is the first edition, dated 1911, of Antonio Casabianca's *Guida Storica del Chianti,* his history of Chianti. Now it's yours." I accepted it from him, speechless with gratitude. He seemed to understand; for the moment he released the book into my care, he warmly slapped my shoulder. We were colleagues; we were friends.

Chapter 17

9 October 2008

A sizeable crevasse appeared before me, and forced me out of my recollection of days gone by. I was just able to leap over it, but I made a note to try a slightly different route on the way back.

I had passed through several woodlands, crossed valleys, and mounted a series of hills, that left me very far from the main roads. Along the way I had collected a few chestnuts that had fallen along with the leaves, and carefully extracted them from their prickly shells. As my pouch was already filled with arbutus fruits and the precious *cucco,* I placed them in my knapsack.

It was now dusk, and the waning light revealed to me, just in time, an abandoned *podere* not far off that I might use for shelter. I reached it just in time to enjoy a brilliant crimson sunset that spilled across the entire territory, setting the glorious fall colors aflame.

The roof seemed sound enough, so I entered. There was little light to be had inside, but I could make out the broad outline of a door, which I pulled from its hinges and placed on the floor before the fireplace, so that I might have a place to lie—the floor being encrusted with the dry and odourless excrement of bats and owls. Then I gathered some olive logs that I was fortunate enough to find piled in the stable, and lit a fire in the hearth.

After unrolling my sleeping bag on the old door, I went to draw some water from the well and poured it into a small tin that I positioned above the flames. Having castrated the chestnuts with my penknife, I tossed them into the boiling water and uncorked a bottle of wine, and treated myself to a long swig. While the chestnuts boiled I sharpened some sticks to serve as skewers; and when I saw there were sufficient embers I slipped the sausages onto the spit. As they roasted I consigned the fat to the flames, causing them to sizzle.

I then minced the *cucco* mushroom, crushed a clove of wild garlic I'd dug up in a meadow along with some rosemary I found growing wild along the wall of the house, and added to these a drop of extra virgin olive oil I'd carried with me. Every now and then the wind would change direction and skitter down the flue, causing a sinister-sounding whine and making the flames flicker and squeal.

As I dined, I tried to imagine how one of the sumptuous city restaurants would describe my humble repast on its menu:

Antipasto: Carpaccio of rare Tuscan mushroom served with wild garlic and herbs, flavored with a hint of stone-pressed extra virgin olive oil.

Primo: Organic chestnuts boiled in authentic Tuscan well water.

Secondo: Cinta Senese pork sausages roasted over olive wood embers.

Dolci: Fresh wild arbutus berries, hand picked in the uncontaminated highlands of Chianti.

Vino: An organic Sangiovese wine produced with grapes picked, pressed, fermented, and drawn from the vat by the master of the vines, Ultimo Gori.

After my dinner I settled down on my improvised bed; it was stiff and uncomfortable. As there was no glass in the windows, gusts of humid winds would occasionally rush in, raising dust mixed with ashes that I couldn't avoid breathing in. Small bats, or "mice angels" as Ultimo laughingly called them, flew in and out of the room hunting for insects. Behind the beams, I spotted a handsome horned owl completely indifferent to my intrusion. With the flames dimming and darkness taking possession of the room, I suppressed my sleep by returning to the avenues of memory. So where were we?

Chapter 18

Getting to know Ultimo

Ultimo and I spent what remained of that day conversing excitedly about Chianti, without ever again mentioning the mysterious *signore*. In truth I almost forgot him, so rapt was I as I spoke—for the first time to someone who truly understood—of my deep affection for the territory in which we both lived. Throughout it all I was conscious of Ultimo contemplating me, taking my measure. He continued pulling books from his collection, in so random a way that I knew he wasn't out to make a point or prove a thesis; he was simply sharing his enthusiasm.

He was, he told me, fascinated by the way this decidedly poor land had been able to attract, over the course of centuries, so many different peoples from so many different places all over the hemisphere. He was equally intrigued by the surprising number of celebrated figures who had first seen the light of day here—a disproportionate number of geniuses and leaders, given the sparseness of our population. And each time he spoke the word "Chianti," it seemed that his turquoise eyes glowed with an inner brilliance.

Every now and then he would remember to add a log to the fire, and would arrange it on the shimmering husks of its predecessors with a pair of tongs. But mostly he talked—and poured wine—and talked some more. He spoke of the Etruscans, and the Romans who claimed this land from them, and the successive Lombard invasions, and the epic struggles between the republics of Siena and Florence, and the castles that sprang up all over the hills like mushrooms after an autumn rainfall.

He never flagged, and there were no awkward silences. In fact his words seemed to be in a race to exit his mouth. He leapfrogged between time periods, jumping from the Renaissance to the Templar cavaliers, to the lives of the sharecroppers, to the Napoleonic troops. He came back, many times, to the wartime era of his own youth, and how it was followed by a near-abandonment of the province as agriculture waned, only to be repopulated by the emergence of tourism as an economic force.

I remained with him until sunset, enthralled by his huge store of knowledge and history. That night, at home and in bed, I began flipping through the book he had given me, and found on its inner cover a dedication in fading ink: *To the esteemed Count Terrosi,* followed by the signature of the author, Antonio Casabianca.

From that day forward, Ultimo became my tutor. I returned to him daily, and my "lessons" ran from weeks to months…and finally to years. Shortly after we started, we began the habit of taking long walks, in all seasons and in any kind of weather, and he patiently pointed out for me the flora, the fauna, the techniques of cultivation, the geological variations, the different types of terrain. He taught me how to make the soil fertile, how to plant vegetables following the waning and waxing moons, how to prune the vines and olive trees, and how to graft fruit trees. In the meantime I continued in my job at the winery; but I devoted each weekend to my real life's work at the *Macie,* with my "maestro," as I called him. He seemed never to age, although I knew he must be getting on in years; he was still very powerful, and his mind still razor sharp—as though he were drawing vitality from the earth of Chianti itself.

As a result I didn't pass my teenage years as a normal youth would have; but then I hadn't really done so prior to my

encounter with Ultimo. I'd left school at fifteen and immediately gone to work. I didn't have any buddies or girlfriends
as would have been normal. Ultimo had been right to see
something unique in me; a gap to be filled. Now I worked
hard at the cellars, then raced home to study the texts he
assigned me. Come Friday, I'd jump on my Vespa and race
off to spend the weekend with him at the *Macie,* often staying overnight. Together we'd comb the woods for Etruscan
tombs, pay visits to castles or villas that had belonged to our
Chianti forefathers, and tread fields that had been enriched
by blood during the epic battles he described to me in such
riveting detail.

I helped him cultivate his vegetable garden and tend his
vines, and if the weather were inclement we'd sit before his
fireplace drinking his wine and smoking. Not once did we
enter a bar, dine out in a *trattoria,* or accompany each other to a village feast. Our friendship did provoke quite a lot
of hilarity in the hills; snide rumors sprang up like weeds.
The grumpy old hermit and the long-haired hippie, always
tramping hither and yon—of course we were the subject of
mirth. We looked like vagabonds, and the difference in our
years perplexed people; what could we possibly have in common?

What they couldn't know is that we shared two great pas-
sions: one for Chianti, the other for solitude. It might seem
a paradox that two men who prize their time alone should
spend so much time together, but because we recognized in
each other this respect for privacy, we felt no threat of com-
mitment from one another—we walked side by side, but not
arm in arm.

I was also quite attracted by the obscure side of Ultimo;
beyond doubt he harboured secrets, impossible to decipher—
secrets that plagued him even as he filled his heart with the

joy of each new day. I knew I would one day learn what he hid; but it would be a privilege, and I would have to earn the right. In the meantime, the contents of the envelope and the mysterious *signore* who had passed it to him through me, were subjects we left untouched.

At the age of twenty I did begin my career as a tour guide, and following Ultimo's suggestions I limited my groups to no more than four persons at a time. He was insistent that I choose to conduct only those who I thought had the seed of real passion for the land, those I considered might be worthy of seeing it so intimately; he would never grant his approval to exposing Chianti to the glares and stares of busloads of fractious tourists. I understood his point entirely, and had never even considered such exposure.

Ultimo continued in his isolation, and never allowed me to bring my guests to visit him, as I had once suggested. Only with me did he manage a healthy, enduring human relationship; he had no desire, absolutely none, to encounter any other living person. I respected this and did not raise the issue again. As my new life became crowded with people, I must have changed in some way; exposure to so many different and often strange individuals can't but have altered me in some degree. And yet Ultimo remained as faithful to me as ever; he still took the time to cook delicious meals with the produce he cultivated and the game he hunted. He never scolded me nor even raised his voice after our initial introduction. He accepted and approved of me for the man I was, something no one had done till then, and it was this above all that kept me devoted to him.

Then one day, after a long walk, he proposed that we go on a week's journey together. He wanted to introduce me to a special place. I instantly understood that this would turn out to be an exceedingly revealing event.

Chapter 19

10th October 2008

I was awakened from my rough sleep atop the doorframe by a cackle of starlings. A wet chill had seeped right through to my marrow during the night, and the fire was long dead. I took a deep breath for courage and pulled myself from the sleeping bag like a silkworm from its tegument. I put on my boots, then got up and went shivering to the nearest window. On its glassless sill lay a scorpion, drinking in the first rays of sunlight. I tapped it with my fingertip to brush it away; at my touch it raised its poisonous talon in self-defense, and hunkered down—it wasn't going anywhere. I decided against a second try.

In the distance I could make out the medieval towers of Siena, and I stood for a while studying the ruddy city as it appeared in the light of dawn. Closer in, a thick haze clung to the valleys, making them look as if they were drowning in a sea of cotton. I turned and retrieved my things, slung my knapsack over my shoulder, and headed out the door to resume my journey.

Outside I paused to breakfast on wild apples and semisoft persimmons I found on the premises, then freshened my palate with some sage leaves I tore from a thriving bush. I then departed the property, leaving it again in eerie isolation; how odd to think that until recently, it teemed with life—generations of families leading self-sufficient lives here, side by side. Now nature had reclaimed it, and was slowly and inexorably swallowing it up. Exposed to the elements like this, it would eventually be rendered a heap of stones, with nothing to indicate human beings had ever lived there.

I had a long day awaiting me; my plan was to reach my second shelter before nightfall and then, the following day, to arrive at the destination to which Ultimo had sent me. I snapped up some porcupine quills I found alongside the way, and while I was bent over, a yellow deer leapt past me so that I nearly keeled over with surprise. A moment later it vanished in the thick forest.

I collected more arbutus fruits, chestnuts, and wild apples as I made my way ever deeper into the most remote area of Chianti. And as I trekked, I remembered...

Chapter 20

3rd October 1994 - Morning - Departure

Ultimo had chosen the day of departure, and informed that on our return he would begin immediately harvesting the grapes, which gave me an idea of how long we would be away. The timing wasn't ideal for me; the tourist season was still in full swing and I was forced to turn over to a fellow guide several groups who had reserved my services. I felt slightly guilty about it, but I knew I'd made the right decision.

The weather was unremarkable on that morning I reached the *Macie* and found Ultimo at the window beaming benevolently at the rising sun. When he saw me he waved to indicate he'd be right down. He closed the shutter behind him and a few moments later he appeared on his stoop, a sack tied with rope slung across his back, his rifle case resting on his shoulder, and the cartridge belt cinched around his waist. *"Ciao, nini,"* he said, and proceeded to tick off a list of items he wanted to make sure I had with me. When he was certain I hadn't forgotten anything, we set off.

The first half-hour or so we moseyed along in silence, taking in the countryside as we'd done countless times before. Eventually we paused so that Ultimo could light a cigarette. He took a puff, then exhaled voluminously. I realized he was now anxious to begin talking.

"Nini," he said, keeping his eyes fixed before him, not on me, "how many years since we first met?" Before I could answer, he said, "Eleven. So I think perhaps it is time for me to tell you more about myself—more, anyway, than you heard

from a certain person when he regaled you with the history of my ill-fated family." He swallowed nervously as if trying to decide how to begin. I held my breath; I'd been awaiting this moment for years.

Chapter 21

3rd October 1994 - Ultimo commences his narration

"The day of my delivery into this world—the second of July, 1908—was also by chance a day of joy for Count Terrosi and his wife, as their sole child, Lorenzo, was born as well. But the Count did not share his joy with his neighbors; the boy was kept jealously within the castle walls and on no account was anyone allowed to see him. The only news regarding the child—who was called the "young count," the *conticino* among the *mezzadri* families—came from the Terrosi servants, and there was little enough for them to tell. The boy lived in a kind of gilded cage.

"Years passed. When I turned six, it became my task to accompany the sheep to pasture. Despite having to endure all varieties of inclement weather, I recall these days fondly; I was young and carefree, the Great War hadn't yet broken out, and I was often accompanied by my sister Carlotta, of whom I was very fond, although she was always in a kind of dream-world of her own. While I tended the flock she picked flowers and pranced about on her toes like a *prima ballerina* at La Scala. When the heat sizzled, and we happened to be close to a creek, she would without a trace of shame shed her clothes so that she was as naked as the day God made her, and splatter about until her skin was wrinkled. Then she would dry herself in the sun and go off in search of honey in the woods. Despite all the bereavements and responsibilities I was burdened with, I still possessed the sensibility of a child, and I was happy to pass my days thus—which was fortunate, because my family could not have spared me from this duty.

"My father was in the first stages of what would prove to be irreversible alcoholism and I had no relationship with him whatsoever. He avoided me, scarcely even spoke a word to me—though by that token he also, fortunately, never beat or even scolded me. My mother too seemed unable to show me affection, probably due to having suffered so much grief that she subconsciously would not allow herself to grow too fond of me, lest I too be plucked away from this world. How could one blame her?

"One day, when I was eleven and we had buried Delfino, Tancredi and Ricciotti, I was tending my sheep as usual when I was approached by none other than Count Terrosi himself. He had been hunting, and was followed by his attendants and hounds. He drew close to me, and I looked up at him astride his imposing bay stallion. I had seen him not more than a few fleeting moments in my life, and had heard only terrifying accounts of him. I was paralyzed with fear before this great figure, imprinted with all the virtues of nobility and clad in rich riding clothes. He regarded me with steely eyes from beneath his felt hat, looking down his convex nose at me, past his cinder-white beard and handlebar moustache. With my hands clasped behind my back and my head hung low in submission, I felt him appraising me, as though I were a heifer.

"'Ultimo Gori,' he suddenly intoned, 'your master *padrocino* Lorenzo and yourself are exactly of an age; did you know that? Yet he is an only child and thus requires a playmate with whom he can amuse himself. On Saturday you may present yourself at the castle.'

"He had thundered this offer as though it were a biblical commandment, then spurred his horse and went galloping away, followed by his men and his baying English setters.

"Do you realize what this meant, *nini?*...I had been invited to Castello Susi as a guest! No *mezzadro* had ever been so honoured as to cross that noble threshold for any reason but service. My parents, when I informed them of the invitation, did not believe my story. Carlotta could offer no confirmation, for while she had witnessed my encounter with the count from afar, she had already forgotten it. Eventually my persistence convinced them I was telling the truth, and Giuseppina, ever adorable, was the first to caress my head and kiss my cheek.

"It was she, too, who woke me with a hug on Saturday morning, her long, loose hair tickling my face. She took it upon herself to scrub me thoroughly, combing my ragamuffin hair and rubbing me with dried lavender corollas. She made me wear a linen shirt I had inherited from Tancredi, sewn up and full of patches; a pair of worn trousers that had come down to me from Ricciotti; and a pair of wooden clogs my father had carved for Delfino from a poplar tree he had felled near the river.

"My mother dispensed a thousand words of advice, among them: to answer politely, not to pick my nose, to thank my hosts, and to bring them the regards of the entire Gori family. And then I walked the seven or so miles that separated the *Macie* and the castle— apprehensive but at the same time ecstatic, as I had only ever seen that august residence from afar.

"It was surrounded by imposing walls, past which lay a lush park with a well-manicured thicket. I passed through the wrought-iron gate surmounted by the family coat of arms, and trudged up the long parkway bordered by cypress trees and clipped rosemary hedges. At the end of the avenue I came upon a series of fountains in which sculptures of mythological creatures spewed water from their mouths, refreshing the slightly stagnant ponds.

"Beyond these was a lush prehensile Tuscan garden, such as was all the rage in those days. It opened onto a rose bed lined with Turkish oaks, willows, cedars, and lemon trees planted in terracotta vases which in winter months would be removed to the safety of the *limonaia*. Tangles of wisteria vines wrapped around chestnut poles tied together by wires. In a corner of the garden stood a gazebo, on whose railing was perched a peacock and under whose roof were caged a riot of richly hued parrots, who at the sight of me unleashed a series of deafening shrieks.

"The castle itself had over the centuries lost the austere aspect of the original military fortress and had, by means of additions and improvements, been transformed into a magnificent country villa. The walls were plastered a faint *terra di Siena* and the windows were festooned with pots of mauve petunias.

"A double staircase conducted me to the main doorway. I began my climb, bewitched by the unrelenting beauty of the setting in which I found myself, and at the same time intimidated by my own unworthy incursion into such majesty.

"I tolled the bell, and the door was summarily opened by a servant named Sandro. He conducted me into the grand entry hall, which was crammed with mirrors and with paintings of hunting scenes in gilded frames. A crystal chandelier dangled from the high, frescoed ceiling. At the far end of the hall stood a luminous white marble staircase with a gleaming brass railing, and a huge terracotta urn resting on the landing. I had never seen anything like this before—an interior that seemed as large as the outdoors itself.

"We did not, alas, ascend the staircase as I had hoped; instead Sandro took my hand and gently led me into an adjoining corridor. The walls were hung with tapestries and portraits of noble ancestors, and other depictions of the glorious past of the Terrosi family. The floor was covered with a carpet of such rich carmine it unnerved me to tread on it; it seemed disrespectful.

"We arrived at a room choked with sofas, armchairs, polished coffee tables and a card table covered in green velvet. Seated on one of the settees was an elderly lady, sipping a cup of tea from a hand-painted porcelain cup. Sandro announced me and almost immediately vanished, leaving me alone with this apparition of age and privilege. It was not my place to speak, but even if it had been, I would not have been able to. I could scarcely breathe, let alone speak. The Countess gave me a glimmer of a smile, then donned a pair of tortoise-rimmed spectacles, gave me a thorough once-over as her son the Count had done, and took up a small plate laden with shortbread pastries and presented it to me.

"'Take one, Ultimo.'

"I remained completely immobile.

"She chose a chocolate-covered biscuit from the plate. 'Take it, go on.' She held it out to me. 'The chocolate are my favorite; so *deliziosi.*' Her voice quavered on the final word, in the way of the aged, but the warmth of her enthusiasm bled through; and I was emboldened to take the biscuit and consume it, almost swallowing it whole. Its buttery sweetness almost intoxicated me.

"The Countess watched me with pleasure, then said, 'Come closer, child.'

"I took a few hesitant steps forward, and when I was within reach she lifted her cold, dry hand and stroked my cheek. Her fingers shook as she did so, and I could feel the stones of her various rings scrape gently against my face, and the hard shell of her lacquered nails.

"'Your eyes are very beautiful,' she said. 'So deeply turquoise! You're a bit too thin, though. Help yourself to another cookie.' She took up the plate again and directed my gaze to a pastry with canary-colored frosting. 'Try the vanilla next…go on, take it. I know you want to…there! Lovely, isn't it?…Ultimo, my grandson Lorenzo is a bit lonely. Sandro has gone to fetch him, so that you can make friends with him. Will you do this for me?…You do know he was born the same day as you? You are coetaneous.'

"I made a ridiculous effort to nod respectfully while still cramming the cookie into my mouth. I knew my mother would have been appalled by my manners. Thinking of her, I remembered that Lorenzo's mother had died mere days after his birth. Even the wealthy were not immune to misfortune. I felt a sudden flourish of commonality with Lorenzo.

"Then the double doors opened and Sandro conducted him in. He was a small-framed boy, almost puny, with a blank, pallid countenance, despite which he was dressed in a jaunty sailor suit with a blue pompom atop his head. His polished leather boots dragged across the floor until he was directly in front of me; then he turned his hazelnut eyes on me with a look that betrayed both curiosity and longing. A moment later he raised his bonnet, revealing a head of shiny, oiled brown hair, and kissed me on the cheek, a move so unexpected that I blushed with embarrassment. His *nonna* smiled benevolently and exclaimed, 'Bravo, Lorenzo!' in her trembling manner. 'Now why don't you take Ultimo to your room and show him your toys?'

"He took my hand—his fingers were as warm as his *nonna*'s were cold—and guided me out of the room, and through a number of long, large halls. One of them housed the most massive fireplace I'd ever seen, a granite cavern above which hung two silver swords, crossed so that their blades formed an X. Another hall was arranged around a huge, black grand piano. Everywhere I looked there was something to astonish me.

"Then, to my delight, we found ourselves back at the entrance hall, and at the gleaming white staircase I so longed to climb. Up we went, the skylight above flooding the marble with such luminescence, it felt like I was swimming in milk. On one of the higher floors, Lorenzo took me down a smaller and humbler hall to his room, which was crowded with wooden toy boxes, brimming with every imaginable diversion from train sets to marionettes; and in the center of the room, a proud, heroic looking rocking horse.

"It didn't take much time to break the ice. Since we were both children, the social distinctions decided on and enforced by adults meant little to us. And as he shared his wealth with me, the blank look on Lorenzo's face faded, to be replaced by a more animated countenance; soon, he was even smiling.

"He invited me to ride the rocking horse, then apportioned me half of his tin soldiers so that we might be opposing armies in mock battle, and introduced me to a game in which interlocking pieces of colored wood were joined together to form a picture; 'a puzzle', he called it. By the time Sandro appeared with two steaming cups of hot chocolate and two slices of cream pastry cake, we were fast friends.

"Later in the afternoon, Sandro brought me back to the Countess. 'Bravo, Ultimo,' she said, beaming at me through her mass of elegantly powdered wrinkles. 'You have made us all very happy today.' And she presented me with a basket of fresh fruits for my mamma, and gave orders to Sandro to take me home in their horse and cart. As I left the room, she said, 'We look forward to seeing you again tomorrow.'

"And thus a new life commenced for me, *nini*. After a few weeks, when it became apparent that my presence at Castello Susi would continue to be required, my shepherding duties were reassigned to the son of the *mezzadri* of *podere Stella*. And in due time I became more than Lorenzo's playmate;

I also joined him in his lessons with his private tutor. Each morning we would study under Maestro Furini, an extremely rigorous yet patient old man, wizened and spindly legged but possessed of a good heart. First I learned to read and write; then came history and geography, and I realized there was an entire world outside the *Macie.* I learned addition and subtraction and even the basics of Latin and French.

"The lessons were conducted in a library of quite staggering proportions, with a dizzyingly high ceiling and walls covered with richly framed maps and ancient documents. At lunchtime I was separated from Lorenzo, and ate my meal with the maids in the kitchen; but after the *dolce* we were reunited, and were free to disport ourselves freely in the garden. There was a labyrinth there, in which we took delight in deliberately losing ourselves. We also mercilessly mocked the gardener, Sante, an ignorant and angry man who I am certain despised me. He did, however, have a gift for cultivating the most blazing roses.

"After our recess we returned to the library and continued our studies. Twice a week a *signorina* would come in to instruct us on the grand piano. You can imagine how dramatically my existence was altered; yet I knew I must remain humble. I was being given the kind of education required to live in the greater world, yet my destiny was to remain forever at the *Macie.* And despite the privileges I enjoyed, I must always remember I was a guest of the family, Lorenzo's chum, nothing more. Adding to my humility was the gratitude I felt; the Countess would periodically send me home with a small sum of money to compensate my time, which she knew was of value to my family. She was surely informed of the condition they were reduced to: an ailing *nonna,* an alcoholic *babbo,* an overworked *mamma* who had to look after the fully grown but in many ways childlike Carlotta, and Giuseppina as the household's sole help mate.

"I also knew that despite the kindness and hospitality of the Countess, I was never truly accepted by the Count himself. He never considered me worthy of even so much as a greeting, and it was by his dictate that I was kept from the family table. It was obvious that my visits had been the desire of his mother, for the benefit of his son.

"As I grew more familiar with the Terrosis I realized something unusual about them: they took no part in any religious activities. There were no crucifixes or other sacred artefacts within the castle, and the massive wooden door to the chapel remained mysteriously bolted shut.

"In the midst of all this my relationship with Lorenzo remained idyllic. We reached a point at which we could read each other's minds with just a glance. Every now and again we would quarrel and even come to blows, but we were boys, this was to be expected, and it was always quickly forgotten. I wished I could take him to the *Macie* and show him my world, but I knew this would never be permitted. He was not even allowed to come to the funerals of my *babbo* and *nonna*. Lorenzo himself seemed never to consider going beyond the castle walls, and was happy to remain there in the company of his father and grandmother—even when the former went off on business for months at a time.

"I think it was for this reason—his lack of freedom—that I never envied Lorenzo. I was quite content to visit him every day, and the moment I crossed that extravagant threshold I would leave my anxieties and worries behind me. I did suffer pangs of guilt each night when I returned home, well fed, to find what remained of my family teetering on the brink of starvation because of the shortages. But I knew it was my duty to return always to this world; it was where I belonged. I had been favored by fate and had the privilege of leading two lives—happy-go-lucky *signorotto* during the day, distressed *mezzadro* after dark; yet the latter was the life to which I would eventually return in full, when Lorenzo came of age.

"In fact I often felt it was Lorenzo who envied me. I think he would have liked to see the world beyond his gates, but lacked the confidence to express it openly. But that world, to which he could not go, would soon come to him. In 1922, when we were entering into our manhood, Mussolini took power in Italy. The vagaries and vicissitudes of Rome were then quite distant things to us, tucked away in the Chianti hills where time seemed to trickle, not gush; but though we did not know it, our trajectory had changed, and our lives, which had seemed so fixed, would not be as we imagined."

Chapter 22

That evening, we camped out in the identical farmhouse in which we'd bivouacked years before, and which I had since learned was the *podere Stella*. Once the fire was lit and our improvised beds were rigged for the night, Ultimo told me that this was where Sante Baldacci, the gardener at Castello Susi, had lived. Sante had a son the same age as Lorenzo, too, and the fact that Ultimo, and not Carlo Baldacci, had been designated the playmate of the Terrosi heir, was the source of the bitter hatred Sante felt towards him.

We dined on pheasant—one of Ultimo's kills, brought down with one shot. He collected some herbs, which he added to the boiling pot on the fireplace, which he'd also flavoured with juniper berries. Ultimo surprised me once again as he took up his narrative again, but this time in *ottava rima* or eighth rhyme: a very old Chianti tradition, now lost. I was so taken by his improvisation that I injured myself while cutting my bread, like an idiot. Ultimo bound my finger with a handkerchief and tightened it with such vigor I thought surely either my bones, or his, would break. And he recited some phrases that were to me indecipherable; and when he released my hand, my wound had, incredibly, stopped bleeding. It was as if he'd worked some kind of spell. For a brief moment I was afraid of him, as I'd been all those years before, when he grabbed my shirt collar.

He gave me no explanation, but appeared exhausted; he lay down on his improvised mattress and stared at the hearth. His gaze was calm, though weary. Then he smiled and life came into his eyes again, the same sparkling turquoise that had so delighted the Countess when he was a boy. I have no clue why he chose this particular moment, but he told me that I must always remember to listen to those who know how to think, and watch those who know how to see. "Keep it in mind, *nini,*" he said, and he took up a flask of wine, tipped it toward the crackling flames in a kind of homage, and took a swig. "Wine is an exceptional opera, a great feat that can be ranked among mankind's most important achievements, like the inventions of the Assyrians, the geometry of Euclid, or the philosophy of Plato."

I waited for more, staving off sleep, till I realized by the sound of his breathing that he had departed into the tenebrous night before me. I allowed myself to succumb…

When I roused myself the following morning, I found that Ultimo had not only risen before me but had been very busy. He'd prepared a hot brew from a blend of roots and herbs he'd previously boiled and filtered. He passed me a cup, assuring me that he'd sweetened it with some honey he'd collected from the trunk of a clipped acacia tree he'd discovered. It was delicious.

Before collecting my things, I unwound the bandage Ultimo had improvised, to check my wound. To my astonishment, it was completely and prodigiously healed.

Soon we resumed our walk, heading toward the most remote hills. A wind had risen, the sky had lightened, and the sun dispersed an icy blue light over the countryside. It was just a question of time before Ultimo resumed his narrative, and so I waited for the moment his penetrating voice filled the chill air…

Chapter 23

Ultimo introduces me to Elena

"Fascism sparked an unpredictable wave of enthusiasm that reached even the most remote *poderi,*" Ultimo said as we continued our march. "My father who for years could find nothing to interest him, suddenly stirred. Even Count Terrosi was swayed. It was this singular quality of appealing to both landowners and farmers that made fascism so ubiquitous in the country. Patriotism—and to a certain extent, chauvinistic nationalism—offered the farmers more favourable conditions. Thousands of acres of swampland were drained, eliminating in many areas the scourge of malaria. Children of all ranks were afforded a basic education, and the party even arranged for them to enjoy summer stays at the seaside, where they were housed in specially erected structures called *colonie.*

"For the aristocracy, on the other hand, there was the illusion of finally being able to stand toe to toe with countries that were traditionally more influential. Italy seemed suddenly to have emerged, energetically and with a united populace, from the oblivion in which it had languished, beneath the nominal rule of an indolent royal family and the governance of a slothful oligarchy. Mussolini, by comparison, appeared a divine prophet, one in whom all hopes could be invested; his will power seemed inexhaustible.

"You see, *nini,* even Count Terrosi himself took part in the march on Rome that sanctioned Mussolini's ascent to power. And this despite—it seems incredible today, but it is true—the Terrosis having been Jewish.

"Meanwhile, my double life continued without a break, its two strands—the *podere Macie* and Castello Susi—moving parallel to each other, never intersecting, for a few more years to come.

"Upon the death of my father, Count Terrosi forced us to share the farmhouse with a pair of brothers he transferred from the *podere Bruciagna*. Adelmo and Armido were middle-aged bachelors, and twins as well. They were extremely simpleminded, but were pure of heart and above all hard workers. They arrived on a cold winter morning, clad in woollen skins and shepherd hats, with capes hooked to their shoulders; they looked like figures from a nativity scene.

"My mother and Giuseppina feared having to cohabit with them, because their appearance was so disquieting: crooked frames, bent limbs, and not a full set of teeth between them. But a few days were all that was required to verify that they were completely harmless, and in fact valuable colleagues. But they were not ideal housemates; they rarely washed, and my mother and Pina more than once chased them to the river wielding brooms, and obliged them to jump in, as they were crawling with lice.

"In no time the brothers were filling the *Macie* with gusts of gaiety. In the evenings, Adelmo played the accordion while Armido improvised dances; watching his scarecrow body jerk and sway was truly a riot. Even Pina's appeal—for she was now at her most beautiful—never caused a ripple of discomfort in the house; on the contrary, the twins grew as protective of her as though they were her own uncles, and it became clear that anyone who interfered with her would have to face them.

"Carlotta, too, in her own way grew fond of them, and before long my mother was openly joyful, something I hadn't seen in her for years. In the evenings, I would often amuse myself by trying to teach Adelmo and Armido how to read and write, but they were as hard-headed as green pinecones; each lesson was forgotten by the time of the next. I was forced to give up.

"My presence among the Terrosi was required less of me now that Lorenzo, no longer confined to the castle, was becoming increasingly involved in politics. He spent most of his time in Siena where he frequented the aristocratic political meetings that were so fashionable during those years. The Count was appointed the local fascist *gerarca* and gradually revealed himself as a sort of despot, deprived of any basic scruples. Rumors spread of cruelties he would inflict on those who wavered in their support of the *Duce* or who refused to join the Fascist party. He was now permanently clad in the black shirt and fez of the *fascisti*. Lorenzo, perhaps unsurprisingly, became an executive of the movement and was sent to Florence to study jurisprudence. At which moment my relationship with the family ceased completely. It was 1929 and I was twenty-one years of age.

"I didn't join the party. Armido and Adelmo did, largely to elude the punitive visits of the *squadristi,* who forced those that refused to drink castor oil—both nauseating and humiliating. But I seemed exempt from such treatment. Though Count Terrosi had never favored my presence at the castle, I'm sure that he sufficiently honoured my friendship with Lorenzo to order that I be left alone as long as I remained politically neutral.

"But I rarely visited the village, and when I did had no political opinion to express that might end my untouchable status. Politics did not interest me; I was now once more a full-time farmer, a miserable *mezzadro,* even though I was fluent in two languages and could play the piano. I also had a perception of what was happening in the world, unlike my fellow farmers who took for granted whatever the local fascist *capoccia* shouted in the square. I was approached by the opposition, whose leanings were decidedly Marxist; they were highly literate characters and I felt some affinity for them, for this reason, but they were too indoctrinated for my liking. They could not converse, only instruct.

"So I was content to let events whirl around me while I returned to the pastures with Carlotta, diverting my mind with classic literature in books I had borrowed from Lorenzo. In time I found another interest: a village girl named Elena who was younger than I, and for whom I developed a tremendous passion.

"She was exactly the kind of woman I was looking for: not particularly attractive, but to my eyes enchanting. She was short and slender, her skin snow white, her hair jet black; and there was something oriental in her features that invariably drew the eye. Each time we exchanged glances I felt more certain that she was the one true love of my life. She had grown up like all the girls of that time, practically illiterate but not completely unschooled, and wise in country ways. She was very sensitive and warm and listened attentively and respectfully when I spoke, which I found very encouraging.

"Her father Giangio had been brought up alongside mine, and had become a carpenter; my father had often visited his workshop to borrow the tools he required to carve his crucifixes. Her mother Eva worked at the post office, but was also a talented dressmaker and taught Elena to be the same. They were very attached. But I was determined that she be more attached to me. I had never fallen in love and did not at first realize that what I felt was more than a passing affection. Certainly I was cheerful in her company, but she remained in my mind even when I was away from her, working in the fields. I eagerly awaited Sunday, which with rare exceptions was the only chance all week I had to see her.

"After mass we took long walks around the village's medieval walls. I recited poetry that I composed for her while tending the sheep. I could so clearly envision my future with her; I could see our home, children. The only problem was that I had no clear idea of what role I was to play in the world. Paradoxically, the education I had been so fortunate to receive, was now plaguing me. I was the head of the Gori family and responsible for running the *Macie*—it was my duty to see that the wheat seeds were sewn, the vines cultivated, the olive trees pruned, the sheep tended, the pigs slaughtered, the ham and salami produced for the Count. It was all I had been born for. But my expanded consciousness chafed against such restrictions, easily comprehending that they were little more than a form of slavery.

"I expected that life must hold more for me, and years went by in which I expected something glamorous to happen that would alter the course of my life. And so I continued to put off the wedding that was so eagerly desired by both my family and hers; and I went through my daily rounds in a kind of half-dream.

"Meanwhile, fascism took hold and imparted entirely different utopian fantasies in many of my neighbors. And then something *did* happen, that changed all our lives—but especially those of the Terrosi family."

At this point Ultimo paused and looked at me with great sadness. "Mussolini delivered the first of his unhinged anti-Semitic edicts."

Chapter 24

4 October 1994

Among Ultimo's many virtues was the ability to put into plain words the most complex ideas and explanations, and he drew on this talent now as he described to me the state of Jewish citizens of Italy both prior to and during the fascist era. It all seemed very far removed, not only in time but space, as we trod through a shaded Chianti woodland, but Ultimo soon made it very present, as though it were unfolding before my eyes. As usual, he astonished me by his uncanny retention of dates, names, and events.

"Jews had never been an issue in Italy as they had been elsewhere; in fact they had integrated well into society. In 1902 there were six Jewish senators, and by 1922 the number had risen to nineteen. In 1906 the Prime Minister was Jewish: Sidney Sonnino, who served a second term in 1909-1910. And indeed he was followed by Prime Minister Luigi Luzzatti, also a Jew, who served in 1910-1911. During the Great War, there had been close to fifty Jewish generals, among whom Emanuele Pugliese was the most highly decorated.

"During the ascent of fascism, three militants named Duilio Sinigalia, Gino Bolaffi, and Bruno Mondolfo were killed, and elevated to the rank of fascist martyrs. Three hundred and fifty of their supporters marched on Rome, and more than twice as many enrolled in the various associations that would later give birth to the *Partito Fascista*. Aldo Finzi was nominated the under-secretary of Internal Affairs for Mussolini; Jung until 1935 was minister of finance; Rava the vice-governor of Libia, governor of Somalia, and yet general of the fascist militia.

"There were also many Jewish businessmen who supported the rise of the *Duce*, who himself didn't hide the fact that he had a Jewish mistress. The number of Jews in fascist circles was very high, *nini*, if we consider that Jews accounted for only a small percentage of the country's population.

"Of course many Jews were also members of the opposition, but this again goes to the issue of integration. There was no Jewish reaction to fascism; there were supporters of fascism, and opponents of fascism, who happened to be Jewish. In fact Count Terrosi was impressed by something Mussolini had said, that he had heard firsthand: 'In Italy we make no distinctions between Jews and non-Jews. In all fields, whether religious, political, military or economic, Italian Jews can find the dream of Zion here, in this beloved land of ours.'

"In 1933 a volume of fascist propaganda was released that again affirmed the absence of anti-Semitism in Italy. Can you believe it, *nini*, that one of the first countries to welcome Jewish refugees from Nazi Germany, was Italy?

"But then Mussolini had an epiphany. He realized that it was in his best interest to ally with Hitler, and from that moment he altered his policies to reflect those of the German leader. The first anti-Semitic broadsides appeared, and the *Duce*, in an effort to secure new fascist sympathizers, proclaimed himself the protector of Islam. Suddenly, Jewish politicians were banned from maintaining relations with their German counterparts.

"In early 1938 Mussolini attempted to mask what was happening by confirming again that there was no anti-Semitism in Italy. But the press was already engaged in a racial campaign based on the elevation of the Aryan lineage, and in July of the same year, concurrent with Hitler's visit to Italy, there came the first truly defamatory campaign against the Jews; many others were to follow. These attacks were at last partially supported by the Vatican, which at that time was not wholly averse to what it saw as moderate anti-Semitism.

"It was from that year forward—1938 to 1943—that racial laws were put into force, that subjugated nearly 500,000 people. Jews were even denied the right to study. The Terrosi were cut down in a series of lethal strokes. Though Fate was kind enough to spare the aged Countess such mortification; she died before she could become a victim."

Chapter 25

9th October 2008 - 4th October 1994

I was making my way under familiar skies, tramping the identical path I trod in Ultimo's company so many years before and breathing the fragrances I inhaled in 1994. The season was the same; even the temperature was similar. The only difference was that this time I was alone; but I could feel a kind of gossamer, fairy-like thread that pulled me back in time, so that Ultimo's voice resounded in my head, almost as though he were next to me.

So it's perhaps understandable that I chose to spend the second night at the same refuge Ultimo chose for us on that earlier trek. Being there again rendered my memories even more vivid; in fact they spewed forth like lava...

The *podere Stella* we had used the night before was a palace by comparison; this was no more than a platform wedged in the branches of an oak tree. To reach it I was obliged to clamber up some rusty stakes driven at intervals into the trunk. Ultimo had erected it himself, he said, for when he hunted squabs, and he assured me of its solidity; but I was wary of the way it shifted under my weight. It was covered by a tarpaulin, but had no walls; we were open to the wind. Lighting a fire was out of the question, and at dusk, in the fall, it can get nippy in Chianti.

Ultimo lit a candle and sliced a salami and some rye bread; from a paper wrapping he produced some *morello* olives he had cured in sea salt. The bright moonlight, sweetened by a veil of translucent clouds, spilled over our heads and combined with the reddish candle flare so that we basked in warmth and light. After dinner, Ultimo lit a cigarette and a contemplative mood settled over us. I thought he might speak again, and waited for him to do so. But when he finished smoking he took some wild apples from his knapsack and put them in a pouch, then gestured for me to remain still and got to his feet, causing the plank to tremble alarmingly. Then he clenched the trunk and shimmied down with the easy agility of a feline.

I peered after him and saw him drop silently to the ground. He lowered himself into a crouch at the foot of the tree, and to my surprise, let out a shrill whistle. After a few hushed moments, the bramble patch began to shake and hiss. Then a pack of wild boars emerged into the clearing and surrounded Ultimo.

My heart skipped a beat, but the old man seemed completely at ease. He reached into his pouch and started distributing the apples; when a boar stepped up to take one, he roughly patted its head and snout, and spoke to it in a low voice. He had an especially tactile relationship with one in particular; when it trotted into the moonlight, it revealed itself in a nearly blinding flash as an albino. I was shocked; I had never seen or even heard of a snow-white boar.

"Melchiorre, my beloved," Ultimo crooned at the beast, "how long since I last came to visit you? Can you forgive me?" He embraced the animal's neck and the boar, who by his size appeared a full-grown adult, nuzzled him back in apparent affection and emitted grunts of pleasure. When they released each other, Ultimo emptied the sack onto the damp ground and allowed the herd to graze on the bounty of apples as he returned to the tree and carefully ascended the metal pegs once more.

I was speechless when he sat once more on the plank with me, unrolling his mat. "I met Melchiorre two years ago," he said almost casually. "The albino boar is a rarity; I had never in my life met with one till then." He seemed to imply that meeting with non-albino boars was the most ordinary thing on the planet.

I expected him to provide me with a full narrative of the circumstances under which he had encountered the beasts and how he had earned their trust, but instead he snuffed out the candle and settled down to sleep. I decided not to pester him about it and did the same, pulling a woollen beret over my head to protect me from the cold. I lay awake for a while listening to the grunts and whinnies of the boars, till they finished their feast and returned to the cover of the woods. Then, in the quiet, sleep claimed me…

In Ultimo's company, it had been fun—even magical—sleeping high above the ground in the canopy of the oak tree, but now, on my own, it was an entirely different experience. I felt isolated and vulnerable. But something occurred to brighten the evening: in emulation of Ultimo, I threw the apples I'd collected that morning to the ground beneath the tree (though unlike him I remained safely in the branches above). Then I whistled—not nearly as loudly as Ultimo, so that at first I wondered whether it had done the job. I waited for a while, almost not daring to breathe; but nothing emerged from the brush. With a shrug of disappointment I wrapped myself in my sleeping back and shut my eyes.

Consciousness began to ebb away from me, till a rustling noise brought it snapping back. I sat up and peered through a crack in the plank. Four wild boars were hungrily devouring the fruit: and one of them was the now aged Melchiorre, his unmistakable white coat dappled by brilliant moonlight. Impulsively I shouted his name, which caused the lot of them to stampede away.

I lay back again, my mind racing, and occupied myself by observing the glittering stars and trying to make out the various constellations and planets. Minutes later I was fast asleep.

Chapter 26

5th October 1994 - 10th October 2008

The morning of the 5th of October, 1994, my slumber was shattered by the deafening report of a rifle. I sat bolt upright and found Ultimo calmly replacing his weapon in its leather case, which he had propped up on the parapet of the platform.

"This evening, roasted squab, *nini,*" he announced with a dazzling, almost toothpaste-ad grin—only a splintered incisor and a missing molar marred the perfection of his smile, despite his avowal of never having had a toothbrush anywhere near his mouth. "Collect your things, tonight we reach our final destination." I blinked the last bit of sleep from my eyes and obeyed, then descended the tree with aching limbs; my awkward position on the hard platform hadn't made for the most comfortable night's rest.

We sought out the three pigeons, losing some time trying to locate the exact bush into which they'd fallen. This brought to mind something I'd long wondered: why didn't Ultimo have a dog? In his position it would have been ideal, not only for retrieving his quarry when he hunted, but for companionship and affection during his long, solitary days and nights. Later, after our breakfast of wine and ham, taken while perched on the smooth surface of some limestone rocks, I asked him this very question. He fixed his gaze on me as he usually did, his serene eyes as always reflected in his wry, wise smile.

"*Nini,* I can't have dominion over an animal and compel it to stay with me. I prefer rather that it should choose my company. And in this way I have found all the companionship I need." He lifted an eyebrow, almost teasing me. "Would you like to see?" Of course I was intrigued, and nodded my assent. "Stay where you are, then, and observe."

He unzipped the game bag and took out a squab, still moderately warm, its lifeless head drooping over the side of his palm. He got up and moved a few yards away, then halted, placed the bird on the ground, clapped his hands, and then opened his arms wide, as if in welcome.

Moments later, a lithe little fox sprang out of the undergrowth of ferns, and trotted up to him, its gorgeous pomegranate-hued fur bouncing and its white-tipped tail whisking back and forth. Ultimo got down on one knee and stroked its head between the ears; amazingly, it fell onto its back as household dogs do when they want their stomachs scratched, and Ultimo obliged.

When it was satisfied, it rolled back to its feet. Ultimo took up the pigeon and offered it to the creature, who grabbed it firmly between its jaws. Then Ultimo gave it a vigorous slap on its backside, and it loped merrily back to the woods, delighted with this unexpected bounty.

Ultimo turned to me and laughed at the stupefied expression on my face; then he gestured for me to pick up my things so we could move on. I had just witnessed yet more evidence of the singular virtues of this man, and when I caught up with him he said merely, "Who needs a dog?"

"Have you named this one as well?" I asked in wonderment.

"No, *nini,* this one I have never met before. It was our first encounter." He paused. "Would you like to give him an appropriate name?"

I thought for a moment, aware of the responsibility he had just given me. But I was young, and in the end I said, "How about Baldassare?" because I loved to make him laugh; his eyes would crinkle shut and two little dimples would form in his ruddy cheeks.

I had kept company with Ultimo for many years and remained captivated by his knowledge and sensitivity. Now I was getting to know a new side of his character—a side he kept well hidden, and that presented him in a fresh light. I wondered whether I was in the presence of a sort of sire of Chianti, a satyr of the woods, a faun in possession of nearly mythical powers. It seemed crazy, but I was also conscious that the surprises he had in store would very likely not end here.

As I recalled that remarkable morning, years later, as I roused myself on the same wooden plank, it didn't seem crazy at all. I yawned and stretched, and looked about me; in the light of dawn I could take in a breathtaking 360-degree vista that incorporated the endless bounty of Chianti in all its magnificence. I couldn't spot even the slightest evidence of human activity; not a cultivated field, a vineyard or village, not even a rooftop. Yet this was the center of Italy, just a few hours' drive from the heart of industrialized Europe. I was completely surrounded by a dense forest of oaks, chestnuts, white acacias and pines.

Above me was an equally dense sky, clustered with cirrus clouds. I didn't possess the highly refined perceptions of Ultimo or Carlotta, but all the same I knew what *that* meant. I donned my hooded rain jacket and started to descend. In the morning light I could see that the plank on which I'd spent the night was now almost rotted through; in another year or so it would collapse, and the soil would eventually reclaim it, and even this rudimentary artifact of man would disappear from the landscape. By then Ultimo would be long gone. But here and now, he was very present in my memory, and once again my thoughts flew back to our epic journey...

Chapter 27

1942

I proceeded at a dreamy pace, making my way through the dense brush with my head hung low, paying little attention to my route. It was a particularly arduous area to tackle, but my mind was occupied in sorting through the events of the wartime period Ultimo had begun to describe to me. Italy was then beginning its decline and disintegration. Mussolini was possessed by delusions of omnipotence; he allied with Hitler and declared war on Britain, and sent troops to North Africa, Albania, Greece, Yugoslavia, and France. It was a shameful waste.

Many young Tuscans were enlisted and sent to the various warfronts. After a few ephemeral victories against British battleships in the Mediterranean, the first aerial strikes by Allied troops over Genova took place, followed by defeats in Africa and at El Alamein. The Italian army, poorly equipped and imperfectly trained, possessed none of the patriotic vigor the Fascist regime was able to create at home. Even the occupation of Greece, which had appeared to be an easy victory, ended in unexpected defeat. Despite this, the Fascist propaganda machine proclaimed victory after victory. But when news of the losses trickled in by word of mouth, discontent spread like an oil stain.

In Spring, Italy lost most of its territory in eastern Africa, and compounded the disaster by participating in action on Russian soil. The ARMIR corps was sent to certain defeat, which ended in an ignoble retreat the following year—a colossal trounce.

Ultimo fortunately was exempt from the call to duty, as he was the sole male child of a widowed mother. The situation in the village, meanwhile, became uncomfortable to say the least, and he decided to leave the *podere Macie* as little as possible. Armido and Armando were too old to be called and continued their labours with unrelenting verve. In comparison with the turmoil and tumult elsewhere in Italy and in the world, it wasn't that bad—though just a few miles off, Count Terrosi couldn't say the same. Following the anti-Semitic edicts he had lost his role as party official or *gerarca*, and was confined to virtual house arrest in his castle, with only the faithful Sandro in his service.

Chapter 28

The return of Lorenzo

"In 1943," Ultimo said, "the German army was crushed at Stalingrad, lost its hegemony in the east, and started its slow retreat, dogged by the Red Army. Before the landing in Normandy, the Axis powers suffered weighty losses in North Africa, and then the Allies disembarked in Sicily. It was just a question of time before the war in Italy concluded; and my family, after so many bereavements in the previous war, had come through remarkably untouched. On the 8th of September the armistice was declared; Mussolini was dismissed, replaced by General Badoglio. The Germans, in a fit of bloody reprisals against the *popolo traditore,* occupied Northern Italy. The country was divided; Mussolini founded the republic of Salò in the north; the south was under Allied control.

"Lorenzo realized he'd better leave Florence, and so returned to Castello Susi. He was distraught at the sight of the glorious garden reduced to a tangle of weeds, and by the imposing halls now barren of paintings, the remaining furniture draped in white sheets. He found his father in the kitchen, a room he had hitherto never as much as stepped foot into; and the old Count greeted his son with both joy and dread. Still uncertain of what his own fate would be, he had now to worry that his son would share it.

"For the Count was caught in the crosshairs: on the one hand, he'd been the *gerarca Fascista* and consequently was now a target for the aggressive communist and anti-Fascist movements, which were joining forces. On the other, he was

Jewish, and was consequently abandoned by his former Fascist comrades, and despised by the Nazi occupiers. He was all too aware of the deportations under way, the combing of the cities in search of Jews, and for the first time in his life he felt what it was like to be on the side of the oppressed. He advised Lorenzo to go and hide at *podere Macie,* to disguise his nobility and mix with the peasantry.

"Accordingly Lorenzo returned to my life the following morning. He spotted me as I tended the vines, ducked behind a bush, and when I passed before it he leapt out and grabbed me from behind. It was a playful ambush, an echo of our boyhood tumbles, but I instinctively feared I was being attacked by a fascist assassin and fought back like a tiger, jabbing my elbow into his stomach, then writhing around and launching myself into him so that we both fell to our knees. I was just about to pummel his face when he looked up and said, 'Ultimo, Ultimo, it's me, Lorenzo!'

"It had been years since I'd last seen him; but now that I looked past his angular, adult face, I could easily see my childhood chum. We embraced, rocking back and forth in joy, then deliberately rolled down the ravine, laughing until our sides ached. When we recovered, we sat and talked, filling each other in on the current situation of our lives. I told him about Elena; he told me that he was now a lawyer, that he hadn't been married or even ever had any serious romance. He had also been an executive of the *Partito Fascista* until, at the time of the anti-Semitic campaign, his resignation was "suggested" by the directive committee, after which his life in Florence dissolved and he had come home.

"When he told me that his father had cautioned him to hide himself among the residents of the *Macie,* I realized that it would be the first time he had ever seen the place, or met any member of my family. And I wondered whether he could do it—live as a peasant, shirking all privilege and social status, carrying his weight instead of being waited on hand and foot. Well, he would have to.

"He was as dry as an anchovy, a sleek, spindle-shaped, elegant figure, with perfectly manicured hands and long, nimble fingers; he probably still played the piano. He was attired in smart travelling clothes, with a waistcoat and cotton jacket. His hair was swept backwards and held in place by abundant pomade, and his moustache was crisply trimmed in the fashion of the time. It would be difficult to hide such a man; his aristocracy was evident from a mile off.

"He didn't seem to realize this. He reported that in Florence a strong partisan resistance was being organized, and it was just a matter of time before Chianti would become part of its campaign to stamp out fascism categorically and forever. He was eager to take part, even enlist in one of the groups. I advised him that while he was staying with me, he should avoid any mention of politics, and to keep in mind that even if his family was the nominal proprietor of the place, it was my home and he must consider himself my guest. My main concern was that he didn't fracture the fragile harmony we had achieved at the *podere,* or bring unwanted attention to us from outside.

"We reached the *Macie* at sunset, and crossed the barnyard, miring our boots in chicken droppings. Once past the threshold we found the family seated around the table before the hearth. 'We have a guest,' I announced. At which Adelmo emptied the spent tobacco from his pipe and, shoeless, padded over to Lorenzo and handed him a welcoming glass of wine. 'I have the pleasure of introducing to you,' I continued, 'Lorenzo Terrosi, the young Count, heir of Castello Susi.'

"My mother emitted a shriek and dropped her head in

an almost instinctive gesture of submission at the sound of the great Terrosi name. Armido, less easily cowed, raised his glass in salute; all the others seemed caught somewhere in between, torn between humility and hospitality. Only Carlotta seemed completely unmoved, as though nothing at all unusual was happening.

"As for Giuseppina, she welcomed our guest with such an entrancing smile that no creature on the planet could have seen it and not been enthralled. Certainly it riveted Lorenzo's attention.

"A great show was made of making room for Lorenzo at the head of the table and filling him a bowl of cabbage soup. I explained that he would henceforth be living with us, at least until the end of the war. I was just about to explain that no favor or respect should be showed him, as he must blend in for his safety's sake, when my mother surprised me by beating me to the punch. She waved the soup ladle at him and in her blunt Tuscan accent said, 'Young man, you are very welcome, certainly; but if you are not here as a guest, then you must earn your keep. There is no room for shirkers or noble titles beneath this roof; we sweat and strain from dawn to dusk, and there will be no exceptions. Now that this is clear you may call me Zia Annita because I will be your auntie, and if you work hard during the day I will feed you well at the end of it. Though judging by your hands," she said, nodding at Lorenzo's smooth palms and fingers, "I doubt you'll be able to contribute much." Lorenzo, embarrassed, quietly hid his hands beneath his jacket, and we all broke into laughter; even Lorenzo himself joined in.

"The succeeding days were strenuous ones for Lorenzo. He had to accustom himself to life without running water or electricity…to sleeping on a makeshift mattress…to using an outhouse with no plumbing. His 'Zia Annita' gave him some well-worn overalls, covered with patches, that had once belonged to my father, Gosto; and he set his fine clothes aside with a sigh. However, he worked diligently and with vigor, and in the evenings, despite his aching bones and chapped hands, never uttered a word of complaint or self-pity; this must be said on his behalf. Over time, I almost became used to seeing my old privileged playmate in the role of a beleaguered *mezzadro*.

"Adelmo sheared off Lorenzo's beautiful hair, leaving him with an efficient crewcut, and Giuseppina made him an ointment to soothe his new calluses. It took only a few days before she herself took to rubbing it affectionately onto his hands. It became apparent to everyone that tender feelings were blossoming between them, and possibly it was due to these sentiments that Lorenzo was instilled with the will to adapt to our lives in the manner we found so laudable.

"You see, *nini*, no one had ever witnessed a nobleman working the fields, much less scooping up pig dung, but Lorenzo did these things with readiness and zeal. He *bustled*. He didn't always do things in the correct manner, obviously, but he did try, and the effort he put into everything he undertook was praiseworthy. It may be that his recent affiliation with the *Partito Comunista* was another reason for his attitude; having experienced the conditions of the working man firsthand, he could despise with even greater cause the fascists who discriminated against him simply because he was Jewish.

"Every now and then he would pay a secret visit to Castello Susi, to verify that his father was well and to sneak in a piano practise. But perhaps his greatest incentive was to listen clandestinely to Radio Londra on the wireless hidden in the loft. On June 4, 1944, the Allies entered Rome and Lorenzo brought the news to us, running with his arms wide and wielding a bottle of champagne he'd nicked from the castle's cellars. We improvised a feast with music and dancing. Adelmo and Armido emptied an entire bottle of grappa and started to hop and skip like lunatics on the table until deep into the night. Lorenzo even managed to get Zia Annita into the celebrations, taking her by the hand and twirling her about like a ballerina. It seemed to us, then, that the war must soon be over."

Chapter 29

5th October 1994

Ultimo and I reached at last our final destination. This turned out to be a small barn, which at first appeared a rather sober, unremarkable structure. When we reached its door, Ultimo took from his knapsack the key that had come to him in the envelope I delivered many years before. He inserted it into the lock and pushed the door open; it squealed in protest. Ultimo entered, and I paused for a moment, savoring the mystery that would soon be revealed. I was not only on the threshold of the edifice, I was on the cusp of achieving the knowledge I had so long sought.

"The foundations are possibly a thousand years old," Ultimo said when I followed him inside; "or even more. But there is no specific front." I looked around. It was, at any rate, a simple barn used to stock bundles of hay. Constructed on two levels, it had a subsided cellar dug into the basement and a demurred yard enclosed by a brick wall—despite which nature was inexorably taking possession. The beams that held up the roof appeared ready to split and bring the whole thing tumbling to the ground.

The place had an enviable vista, though; from this vantage point we had a panoramic view of the surrounding territory, so that both Ultimo and I took the time to turn and take it all in. This was the country that enchanted and captivated us: our beloved Chianti.

"Often, *nini,*" he said when we were once more outside and seated on the wall, with the sun beating on our necks, "while contemplating this eternal view, I have let my imagination go, and fantasized making this the site of my own personal *osteria*. The restoration work would obviously be demanding, but despite the general dilapidation I can see a solid framework here." His eyes roamed over the ancient walls, as they must have done many times before.

"Once the *osteria* is completed, it should appear much as it does now—by which I mean, it should remain an integral part of the territory, as if risen up directly from the soil. As indeed it was; it was built utilizing only materials, principally limestone, that were dug out of nearby fields. I have replaced many of the missing ones myself, with stones I've found lying smoothed and ready from centuries of weather. It amused me to find just the right stones to fit the cavities, like the pieces of a giant puzzle. It made me feel like a minor deity, *nini,* to give back form, and even a kind of life, to these rocky elements; and to give them purpose, too—the sheltering of my proposed *osteria.* I would reject the ones of equal measure in favor of those more irregular—those with character—and run my hands over them, removing the earth as I do to the potatoes from my vegetable garden. I would reinforce the walls so that one wouldn't notice the plaster, giving the possibility of growth to thick dangling caper bushes emerging from the crevices.

"The roof I would like to cover in crimson tiles, like those baked in ancient, family-run furnaces. I would make sure that each had a shading dissimilar from those adjacent to it, so that there would be a chromatic pattern only slightly perceptible to the eye." He was in a sort of trance now, and though he was looking past me, over the hills, I knew he was seeing his imaginary roof, in minute detail.

"I can see the roof covering the two structures, erected on two levels; I would swathe the entrance with a wattle shelter supported by a pair of trunks of our local oak wood, imbued and treated with natural resins that exude the perfume the forests give off only in the months in fall. Vines that alter their colors with the seasons, from pale green to a fiery red, would wrap the shafts, along with ivy that maintains its solemn aspect even during the so-called dead months. I can picture the trusses of the veranda submerged in wisteria, with clusters of mauve flowers dangling all the way down, brushing the heads of the wild blooms. I would not sweep their fallen petals, not even when they were thick on the broad terracotta tiles, until they had withered and gone brown.

"In between the runners of the floor, I would love to see hints of verbena, to seal the amalgamation of nature and structure. On the brick paving I would set square tables made of copper-red beech wood, imperfect and warped, and chairs with straw seats; also a few refectory tables with ample benches: furniture, you see, of humble origin, without pretense, yet robust and pure: in a word, *Chiantigiani.*

"I would brighten up the small well with a red *terra di Siena,* always keeping it filled with fresh spring water, and surround it with shrubs of scotch broom that in spring release that heady, dizzying scent into the air, and delight the eye with their golden flowers."

I sat listening, almost not daring to breathe. It astonished me that this old man's most private secret, the secret he had kept from me so long, was nothing to do with his eventful past: it was instead a brilliant vision of a future.

"At the entrance, my guests would be greeted by a tangle of junipers, rosemary and lavender, so that with every breath the lungs would fill with a profusion of sweet fragrances. To give an extra touch of *Toscanità* I would plant some bent and twisted olive trees, a tall cypress, a fig, a yew, and a Judas tree. In the infracts of the beams, I would love to have swallows build their nests, and to serenade us with their joyous song each spring."

Suddenly he stood up, and I did as well. I followed him back to the barn while he continued his monologue, now waving his hands with passion.

"I can picture the main entry consisting of an ample glass window with an arched vault; I imagine it overrun by a blood-red rose. And inside, the same flooring as the exterior, only properly cured and polished with wax. On the chestnut-beamed ceiling there would be large iron hooks where I'd hang hams and salamis. The stone walls would remain as they are, honest and plain, if not entirely straight—except for one, which I would stucco and whitewash, for the display of ancient tools and utensils used in the past to tend vines and olives.

"The fireplace should be imposing, so large you can actually sit inside on benches. The girder would be fashioned from cypress and the cape surmounted by a bas-relief in terracotta of a rising sun. I would also restore the ancient woodburning oven, in which I would bake bread and *focacce* to be served, still warm.

"The counter would have to be of rustic walnut, placed on a wall of jumbled bricks and stones, next to a refrigerator stocked with wheels of seasoned pecorino cheese. I wouldn't keep bottled wine, only two oak barrels: one for red, the other white, which I would dispense into straw-matted flasks. Behind the counter I would restore the modest archway, and the steep staircase using the original hand-hewn granite steps, leading down the cellar with its barrels and demijohns resting on a loose gravel floor. There I would rest for hours, just to breathe in the musty, stale air, watching as the rocks quietly sweat in the damp."

He turned to me, having momentarily exhausted himself,

but his eyes still shone with ardour. I had no wish to dim his excitement, but before I could stop myself I said, "But Ultimo, who would ever come to dine at a place so far removed from any roads or pathways, so isolated in these hills?"

He shrugged and gave me a half-smile, and said, "Ahh. Maybe you are right, *nini.*"

His flight of fancy finished, he turned to practical matters, directing me to set up my sleeping bag in the area he had judged least unstable. *"Least* unstable?" I asked, eyeing the ceiling dubiously.

"Yes, *nini,*" he said, "for it is likely the roof will collapse this very night!" He cackled as he settled down, and I knew that he was still in a kind of ecstasy. He'd been disappointed by my initial reaction—to him, I'd seen only problems, not possibilities—but I was young. And I would make it up to him tomorrow. In the meantime, I was blissful at sharing this moment with him.

Chapter 30

10th October 2008

As I had predicted, rain came. It started with a drizzle, then the white clouds were driven away by a fleet of black nimbus sailing in like battleships, unleashing a true downpour. I was adequately protected in my impermeable jacket, and I was reminded of a comparable incident that occurred in Ultimo's company in a dense wood. He had pointed out how the contours of the trees appeared more distinctly defined in the storm than they had under the sun that morning. I breathed in and filled my lungs with air that was laced with rainwater. At the same time, pearls of the stuff ran down my oilskin jacket and the wind buffeted me with the scent of stonecrops.

I was inexplicably stimulated by that rainfall—almost inebriated by the saturated air. Enraptured, I felt joy coil within me, needing release, so I lifted my head to the sky and opened my mouth. It soon filled with streams filtered through the leaves of the Chianti forest; I spat it out, then stretched my arms and arched my back, and lifting my voice I shouted with all my might—a sentiment that surprised me, more grieving than joyful, that I had not allowed myself to feel until just now:

"Ultimooooooooo, don't leave me now!"

Chapter 31

Spring 1944

"Weeks passed. Lorenzo had brought a gust of grace to the *podere,* even if he now smelled of manure like the rest of us. His polite *signorile* manners, his easy charm and his aristocratic turns of phrase, subjugated all of us, Adelmo and Armido included. The twins, incapable of uttering a phrase that didn't include a vulgar epithet, enjoyed imitating Lorenzo's inflections and mimicking his gestures, making us all howl with laughter. As for Giuseppina, she and Lorenzo were now a couple. Though they attempted to hide their feelings from Mamma, it was evident to the rest of us; they would bill and coo at every opportunity. Adelmo and Armido not only approved, they invented pretexts to take Carlotta with them when they went about their chores, so that Giuseppina and Lorenzo would have time alone together. In any case, they were both in their thirties and their union could scarcely be forbidden by any of us, even if we wanted. Personally, I was intrigued by the idea of Lorenzo as a brother-in-law. The only person who would certainly object was the elderly Count, both on the grounds that Giuseppina was neither noble nor Jewish. And for that matter the regime itself, which forbade intermarriage with Jews.

"One sizzling morning I went to the village, ostensibly to obtain salt to cure the hams and tobacco for the twins and myself; but really to pay court to Elena, who I hadn't seen for weeks. During the long walk under the scorching sun, I noticed that the hills were swarming with pale purple irises, and the slight breeze made them roll like the surge of waves.

"I entered the village through the main gate, beneath an ancient clock. The alleyways were deserted and the silence was profoundly eerie. I went straight for Elena's home, a small apartment on a shady cobbled lane; I was certain I'd find her alone, knitting and sewing. Her father had died a few years earlier and her mother was out all day, working at the post office. Her older brother was an enlisted man serving at the Greek front, from where they received sporadic news of him—the latest being that he was on the island of Cefalonia in a legion under the command of Captain Corelli.

"The moment Elena opened the door, I handed her a bunch of wildflowers I'd picked along the way, and her joy in seeing me burst from her sweet face like sunlight. She had a foulard knotted under her chin that covered her intense jet-black hair, with the exception of one unruly tuft that tumbled over her forehead. She wore a pearl-white lace shirt and a cinder-grey skirt that complemented the ash-grey of her eyes. She could not have been more beautiful to me.

"She embraced me warmly, and I felt her swelling breasts press against my chest; we kissed with such intense emotion that we were swept away by ardour, hastily shedding our clothing and making love right on the living room couch. Afterwards we clung together, stroking and fondling each other in complete silence. Then we dressed and retired to the kitchen, where Elena made some boiled rice which she served with olive oil.

"We talked about the difficult times, and our upcoming wedding, which we had decided to celebrate as soon as the war ended. She brought me up to date on the situation in the village, how terror ruled the streets, about the rumors of a Nazi contingent that was supposedly coming to lend a hand to the local fascists. I told her that Lorenzo was living with us and how he had unexpectedly taken to his role of *mezzadro,* even to the point of falling in love with Pina. I also reassured her that Mamma and Carlotta were well, and told her how Armido and Armando spiced up our evenings with their dances and buffoonery, and how despite the hard times, we should consider ourselves privileged. I even proposed that she move in with us, and share a room with Giuseppina and Carlotta.

"She feigned to smile and tied the foulard back around her head, then led me to the door, saying her mamma would be home soon and it would be best that I shouldn't be found here alone with her. We kissed goodbye and I promised to return soon; and before departing, I handed her a basket of eggs to give to her mother on behalf of mine, which in my passion at seeing her I had left on the doorstep.

"Again I was alone on the empty streets. The sense of terror must indeed be great, to keep so many people indoors on such a fine day. For my part I felt only euphoria; Elena was the ideal woman, and she was mine. I headed for the gate of the village, but my pleasant thoughts were interrupted when I passed a local bar where a group of fascists were tossing back shots of white vermouth. When they spotted me, Sante (yes, *nini,* the old gardener of Castello Susi) called out, 'Look who's here, the friend of the Jews!'

"A second voice, belonging to a young bumpkin named Eugenio Fanti, son of the village notary, chimed in: 'Not only that, but a deserter, the son of a drunk and of a mother who whelped a bastard son."

"Impulsively, I whirled on them, and Eugenio added, 'Pina, the Etruscan, ain't bad either—a splendid whore.'

"I was just about to give in to frenzy; but a bit of the calm I had gained with Elena allowed me to regain control. I believed it was best not to grant those *idioti* satisfaction. I turned away.

"Then Sante, looking lumpish in his fascist squadron uniform with a black fez perched on his ape-like brow, swallowed another glassful and barked, "Your sister Carlotta may be deficient, but she does us great service when she frolics naked along the river." And it was this, the smear on innocent Carlotta, that made me snap and fall into their trap.

"'Maybe so,' I said. 'But I think you service yourselves even more satisfyingly. We all know where you like to sheath those batons.'

"There was a moment of deadly silence, in which I realized I'd committed an unmitigated folly. But running away wasn't in keeping with my character; and in any case, they'd surely have caught me. All I could do now was stand my ground and face them.

"I rolled up my sleeves and positioned myself in the middle of the square, my back to the old town hall. For a split-second, my gaze was caught by the image of the suffering Christ under the church's lintel. The heat was at its peak; sweat bonded my shirt to my skin, and the only sound was the soft gurgle of the fountain in the center of the piazza. I sensed many eyes behind many shuttered windows, but I knew no one would come to my aid.

"Sante, his face purple and his teeth grinding, got up, as did Eugenio and Poppo; they surrounded me. Poppo was a foolish young man with tight shoulder blades and no neck, who worked as the barber's apprentice. Fascism had given him a phoney sense of prominence.

"'Okay,' said Sante with menace on his tongue, 'you mock our batons?...Then feel their reply on your shit-caked head.' He swung a blow at me which I dodged, delivering an uppercut that landed squarely on his nose, shattering it. He shrieked in pain and covered his face with his hands; blood seeped between his fingers.

"I was about to face Eugenio, but Poppo thumped me on the head from behind, leaving me temporarily vulnerable to Eugenio, who used the opportunity to punch me in the liver, causing me to fall to my knees. While I was down, gasping for breath, I heard the shutters of the few shops still open, banging shut. Then I took a boot in the face, tearing open my gums and filling my mouth with blood, which streamed onto the cobblestones.

"The two thugs kept at me, but then Sante came between us and crouched over me, blood flowing over his face, his nose now revealed as a mass of splinters and cartilage; and he slammed his baton into my abdomen. 'That's for all the fun you and Lorenzo had at my expense. And *this*,' he snarled, raising the baton again, 'is because you're a Jew-lover…and *this* is because you never served your country…and *this* is for breaking my *nose*, you Communist son-of-a-bitch!' And with each accusation, another blow.

"Finally Poppo pulled him away and tried to calm him down; but this left Eugenio free to slice my cheek with his pocket knife. See, *nini*, I bear the scar to this day. And then Sante broke free, pulled his pistol from its holster, and placed it against my forehead. I was by now a mass of blood and pulp, but even through the pain I could feel the cold barrel pressing into my skin. He disengaged the safety and then with his thumb spun the chamber, and put his finger on the trigger. I heard it *click*—and thought, This is it, this is my last moment on earth—

"—but nothing happened. Then there was raucous laughter and Eugenio kicked my genitals, and Sante howled, 'It's unloaded, you sad bastard! I bet you shat your pants, you Communist pig! The next time I see you in town, I'll empty all the lead I have into your ugly face!'

"Then Eugenio fired his own gun into the sky, causing a

flock of blackbirds to take sudden, shrieking flight. And he cried out, 'All you cowards peering out from behind your shutters—*this* is what happens to those who cross us. Remember! Next time we won't be so generous.'

"Then the three colleagues ambled off, drunk on violence, singing the fascist anthem, *'All'armi! All'armi! All'armi siam fascisti terror dei comunisti....'* leaving me half-dead in a pool of my own blood. But before they were out of sight I summoned the strength to salute them with a gesture which, had they seen it, would surely have brought them back to finish me off. Then I fell back into the dust, and tried to breathe as best I could, though each breath was like a knife lacerating my lungs.

"Eventually I lost consciousness, and when I regained it I was back at Elena's house, on the very settee where just an hour before we had experienced such bliss. It seems that some courageous villagers collected me and hauled me back to her on a cart. Her lovely face was hovering over mine; it was her tears dropping onto my face that had awakened me—as well as the invocations of Don Mauro, the young parish priest who had come to us after Don Oraldo died.

"Elena and her mother swabbed my wounds with vinegar and alcohol. By some miracle, none of my bones were broken, although I was from head to toe a patchwork of black and blue bruises. My face was swollen and my cheek flapped open like a can of sardines.

"Don Mauro took me home on his cart. On seeing me, my mother covered her mouth, then burst into tears. In an effort to prove I was all right, much better than I looked at any rate, I boldly made my way up the steps alone, refusing all assistance."

Chapter 32

5th October 1994

Ultimo put me in charge of lighting the fire. I composed a few bundles and snapped some oak branches from a dead tree, while he plucked our remaining two squabs and prepared them for cooking. Then he chopped off their heads and stuffed them with a mixture of rosemary, sage and salt, skewered them, and placed them over the crackling flames in the fireplace.

I couldn't keep my eyes off the scar on his cheek; I had of course noticed it before, but now that I knew its origin it seemed much more prominent. I could only presume that his chipped tooth was also a consequence of that brutal morning in 1944.

From the opening in the roof, we could see the starry vault of the heavens, so pure in substance that it seemed heavenly indeed. I shivered and drew my arms into my trunk; it was colder than average, as an eastern wind was blustering. *"Tramontana* wind tonight, *nini,* our fangs are going to chatter!" my dear friend said with a wink as he chopped some wild salads, which he then dressed with a drop of oil from the glass cruet he always carried with him.

While the birds were roasting, we drew some wool rugs about our shoulders and shared a fiasco of wine, passing it back and forth and drinking directly from the bottle. When he slid the pigeons from the skewers, Ultimo said, "Remember that blame is never all on one side, and whoever answers it with violence shall only create more."

Every time he pronounced something of this nature, he

wore a look so sagacious and yet so affable, that his wisdom seemed more like a gift than a lecture, and resonated warmly in the deepest recesses of my soul. Then he continued: "The judgment of an enemy is often more truthful than that of a friend, because in men, hatred is usually more profound than love. The perception of those who despise you is always clearer than that of those who love you. A true friend is another you, while an enemy is your opposite, and therein lies his strength. Hatred illuminates many things that love keeps in shadow. Remember that, and never despise or reproach your foe, *nini.*"

I had difficulty comprehending the significance of this at first; then I realized he must be talking of Eugenio and Sante. Then, his eyes gleaming, he told me that a local boy, born in these very hills, had first written those words. His name was Leonardo da Vinci.

Chapter 33

June 1944

"The partisans," said Ultimo, his lips shiny with fat as he sucked with relish the squab's black carcass, "had been operating in Chianti, subverting and disrupting the fascists and the Germans—though even today their effectiveness is a matter of debate. Many unruly young men chose to slink away into the woods, and to survive they relied on nearby *poderi.* They had paid multiple visits to the *Macie,* begging for provisions that we never denied them.

"The major problem was that whenever they did pull off an action, the Nazis would retaliate by punishing the villagers, selecting them at random and lining them against the wall of the town hall for immediate execution. For this reason we lived in absolute terror, but we couldn't exempt ourselves from work, as we were obliged to look after the farm animals and reap the wheat on which our subsistence depended.

"During a break in the vineyard, I went to the river to refresh myself and to see what Carlotta was up to; typically I could find her by the sound of her splashing about. When she heard me approaching, she would dress and come up to greet me. As I followed the path to the creek, my arms brushing against the Spanish broom that bordered it on both sides, I had to wave away swarms of honeybees, who seemed to have descended on us *en masse* that year, and for this reason—I was distracted by their buzz and hum—I didn't notice till I reached the banks that Carlotta wasn't alone. My heart leapt into my throat when I saw Eugenio Fanti with her, tormenting her; he gripped her by the arm and was trying to rip off her dress. Carlotta was flailing, but emitted no cries, only a mournful wail.

"I hurled myself forward, berserk with rage. Eugenio didn't hear the pounding of my step, as he was growling his aggression at Carlotta, so he wasn't aware of me until my full weight fell on him, knocking him to the ground. Carlotta ran off, and before the fascist villain could get his bearings I had my hands around his throat; all my hatred and anger were channelled down my arms into my fingers.

"Eugenio wrested his arm away and grasped the wound on my face he had inflicted just a few weeks before, not yet fully healed. This only enraged me all the more; I started banging his head against the pebbled riverbed, strangling him with increased vehemence. I can't recall how many times I smashed his head down, but soon enough his grip on my face slackened. I could feel his life force rushing out of him. His eyes went strangely glossy, and his arm fell heavily beside me, scattering the pebbles. I sat straddled over him, panting like a bellow, sweat dripping from my face onto his chest. At last I released his throat and stared at him; his impassive face seemed, too late, to be asking for mercy.

"I had just taken the life of Eugenio Fanti, son of the village notary.

"As soon as I realized the gravity of my actions, I felt a sudden grief come over me; I was on the verge of tears. I staggered to my feet and dragged his inert body to the river, where the current leads to the bottom of the valley and the water rises to my waist. I pushed his cadaver into the stream and prayed that none of his cohorts were in the vicinity.

"I floated him around several bends, a few hundred yards

to where the vegetation grew denser. There I removed his belt and wrapped it around his ankle, and knotted the other end to the roots of an abele tree.

"I returned to the exact spot where I had committed the crime, my heart still pounding like a hammer. I was nearly overcome with guilt. I have always been a pacifist, *nini,* a supporter of non-violence; but what else could I have done? That man was abusing a defenceless autistic woman—my sister, my responsibility—and would most probably have killed her after he finished with her. Certainly he would have killed me, for having prevented him.

"I grabbed his rifle from the rock against which he had set it and rushed back to the *Macie.* Fortunately, I caught up with Carlotta, who was encircled by a covey of butterflies. She was never a very expressive girl, but even for her, she seemed traumatized—her eyes were blank, her step unsteady. She kept trying to pull her dress closed where Eugenio had ripped it, and repeated the words 'nasty man, nasty nasty man' in a haunting monotone.

"I clasped her hand and hugged her; I caressed her flaxen hair and covered her with kisses. 'Don't worry, sweetie, the nasty man will never return, I promise,' and I kept on reassuring her of this all the way back to the *podere.*

"The first person I saw was Lorenzo, who was cleaning the cages of the few rabbits we still had. His eyes widened; he could tell instantly that something was wrong. I ordered him to go at once and fetch the twins from the wheat field, but he paused to ask me all sorts of questions. I stopped him, telling him he would learn what had happened when I told the rest of the family, when we were all together, and he raced off on his errand. Alas, I couldn't keep my promise to wait for the return of the men, as my mother implored me to relate the incident at once, and her distress was so heartrending I could not deny her. As I explained, Carlotta sobbed in Giuseppina's arms.

"'*Madonna mia,*' Mamma exclaimed, her hands joined in prayer.

"'Nasty man, nasty man,' Carlotta murmured. Pina, however, reacted with uncharacteristic decisiveness. She gently removed herself from Carlotta, dried her hands on her apron, and asked, 'What will you do now, Ultimo? What?'

"At that moment the three men returned. When I told them what had happened, Adelmo burst into a fit of cursing, while Armido paced the room like a panther, his hands behind his back. Lorenzo embraced me and then put his arms around Giuseppina.

"'I have no alternative,' I said, answering Giuseppina's question at last. 'To protect all of you, I must leave at once, seizing the advantage of time before they become suspicious of Eugenio's absence. I must go into hiding, and try to hook up with some partisan cell. I will do my best to send you news whenever possible.'

"I then told the twins to look after the *podere* and not to make the same mistake if ever they were provoked. They were fortunately registered with the Fascist party, so no one should have done them any harm.

"I held my mamma close, and for the first time she told me she was proud of me, and that my *babbo* would have been as well. 'I love you, Mamma,' was all that I could manage to utter. Then I bid a tearful farewell to my sisters; and at the moment of departure, I made another announcement, which took them all by surprise.

"'Lorenzo, collect your things; you're coming too. As soon as they discover the corpse, they'll come looking for me here. And you can't risk being recognized; you're Jewish; the Nazis will arrest you.' Lorenzo's face turned pale, and Giuseppina burst into tears.

"'But what of my father?' Lorenzo asked. 'I can't abandon him this way!'

"'There is nothing you can do for him, Lorenzo; you must save yourself. Come on; collect the essentials. We must go at once.'

"And we all drew together in a pitiful, collective hug."

Chapter 34

5th October 1994 - Night

The hours of darkness brought even more cold; we continued feeding the fire, tossing logs into its maw whenever it began to wane, and watching helplessly as most of the heat swept up the flue. The wind barrelled through the room vehemently, howling like an animal.

Ultimo's mood had darkened as he narrated that terrible episode of his life; but now he brightened, as though he'd freed himself from a great burden. His usual aspect of serenity returned, his childlike pleasure in living simply in the moment.

We kept passing the wine bottle, each time taking smaller swigs, so that in nursing ourselves with tiny doses we could extend the life of the treatment.

Another gust of wind blew over me, and I tugged my beret down over my ears and donned a pair of merino gloves; but it wasn't sufficient to thwart the chill. It had got into my bones now. Certainly the next morning we would awaken to a hoarfrost, an unusual phenomenon for the beginning of October.

It was just as well that I couldn't sleep, because Ultimo seemed to have no interest in slumber. His mind was alive and his eyes bright, and he was eager to continue his story.

Chapter 35

Ultimo and Lorenzo, partisans

"Lorenzo and I were thus driven to hiding in the forest, leaving behind all our friends and family to face an uncertain fate. From that point on we had no way of knowing what was occurring in the world; but our spirits would soar when at night we would spot in the sky the flares from the Allied artillery, and recognize the silhouette of the Flying Fortresses heading south.

"The first week we moved through the brush in search of a partisan group headed by the famous Bruno Bonci, known as Caravaggio, that had successfully operated within the Sienese part of Chianti, and was known to have direct communication with British troops. Alas, we didn't find them, but came instead upon a group of poorly equipped, unruly drifters led by an old friend of Tancredi who I'd seen many times at local village feasts. He had, I recalled, been particularly impressed by the juggling feats of my brother, Ricciotti.

"His name was Massimiliano and his partisan name was Tamburo, or drum, because in his youth he had been the drummer for the Noble Contrada of the Goose in Siena. He was an enormous, stocky man with an impressive black beard, and his massiveness was all the more pronounced as he was accompanied by Gigi, known as Grissino—breadstick—a skinny, delicate young man in his early twenties, the son of a family of *mezzadri*. He'd chosen to desert when he was summoned to join the Fascist army—as had the baker's son, Gianni, whose cascading blond ringlets, like a celestial being in a Botticelli painting, won him the nickname Angelo.

"We came across them while they were bathing in a creek. Actually it had been Tamburo's dog, Benito (so named because he was the son of a bitch) who heard us approaching and began barking furiously. We stepped forth from the forest with our rifles above our heads, shouting our names, declaring who we were. I was recognized instantly, but Lorenzo's identity had to be explained, and our three new companions couldn't at first believe that the *conticino* himself stood before them.

"Tamburo was only too glad to welcome us into his rugged little band, because he had lost three men a week before in a gunfight with German troops. To solemnize our new partnership we presented him with a wheel of pecorino cheese, and when they had dried and dressed themselves we sat down on the rocks and exchanged information—save for Grissino, who went hunting for frogs for dinner.

"Lorenzo revealed that I had killed Eugenio Fanti with my bare hands, which gained me considerable respect in their eyes. Angelo in particular, who had suffered much persecution at Eugenio's hands, proposed a toast to me, but I declined it. For this reason they named me Scrupolo, or qualm, and Tamburo elected that Lorenzo's *nom de guerre* be Noble.

"For the purpose of security, the group had no fixed camp, but moved about during the day, hoping sooner or later to encounter Allied troops. I learned that they had bumped into Bruno Bonci more than once, and that they had set a rendezvous with him for three days hence, at the *Poggio Pini,* the pine hill. In the meantime, food was scarce and Tamburo proposed going to the *Macie* for provisions, but I said this would be complete folly given my current status as the fascist's Public Enemy Number One.

"That night I pulled out my tobacco tin. It had been a long time since I'd rolled myself a cigarette; and when I opened the lid, I discovered a pleasant surprise: a small photo of Elena that she must have slipped in while I was unconscious on her couch. I held the photo, gazing on it as I smoked; then after having kissed it gently I returned it to the tin, placing it in my breast pocket so that it was as close as possible to my heart.

"That night we heard a tremendous din from the north; it was evident the retreating Nazis had blown up a *podere,* possibly even an entire hamlet. From the opposite direction came sounds of artillery blasts, which gave us an idea of the vicinity of the liberating troops. In three days' time, our tryst with Caravaggio would shed light on what was actually going on in Chianti. Till then we were plagued by restlessness, and the echoing roars in the valley made us uneasy, filling us with dread."

Ultimo paused; but I knew he had not finished. The story was unravelling, coming out of him with a force all its own. Neither of us had a watch but I was certain it was well past midnight. Aside from the crackling of the fire, the only sound was the low hooting of a horned owl nestled somewhere close by.

"When we reached *Poggio Pini* there was no trace of Bruno Bonci or his men, though we waited several hours. Lorenzo started to worry; I told him to remain calm, lest his uneasiness infect the rest of the group. I was leaning against the trunk of a cypress; Tamburo stood next to me, Benito next to him, and Angelo and Grissino stood guard, their hands firmly clasped to their rifles, their eyes scouring the valley.

"Suddenly a shot rang out, breaking the stillness, and Grissino dropped to the ground, a rivulet of blood trickling from his mouth. His body quivered briefly, then was immobile. Tamburo shouted, 'An ambush! Run for cover!' The words were still on his tongue when he was hit by a volley of machine-gun fire and died instantly.

"We soon spotted the German patrol and ran in the opposite direction, hoping we weren't surrounded. Angelo was hit—a bullet passed through his right leg, causing him to crumple like a marionette. I braked my sprint and Lorenzo, who was in front of me, turned and shouted, 'Let him be, Ultimo, let's save ourselves!'

"In the tumult, I couldn't but notice that Benito remained beside the body of his ill-fated master. Angelo dragged himself towards the escarpment that led to the bottom of the valley, seeking desperately to save his life. With Benito's loyalty as an example, I couldn't abandon Angelo. I darted over to him.

"'You're crazy, Ultimo,' Lorenzo cried as he reached the bottom of the dale; 'they'll kill you!' He scrambled towards the opposite side of the slope, and the high scrubs that swayed in the wind; salvation was there. When we reached the top there'd be a dense wood into which we could melt. All I had to do was follow him.

"'Help me, Scrupulo,' Angelo wailed; and I turned back to him. What the hell, I concluded; the Nazis were still some way off, and I guessed there to be no more than ten of them. I lifted Angelo's slender body onto my shoulders and hauled him away.

"All I needed to do was to carry him up the ravine, and we'd have a chance at getting away with our lives; but I was well aware that his extra weight would make the climb an epic task. And so it was; my heart almost burst from the effort; my mouth went dry and parched, and my breath came in gasps. Sweat flowed into my eyes, blinding me. And it seemed with each minute Angelo got heavier and heavier.

"Lorenzo, in the meantime, had reached the top of the hill

and taken shelter behind the trunk of an oak tree. This gave him a chance to gather his courage, God bless him, and he began shooting, disorienting the Nazis. Another round of machine-gun fire sprayed the ravine just as I was nearing the top, and I heard Angelo's head burst, bathing me in blood and brains. His right eye fell at my feet and he released his grip, sliding into the high grass.

"'C'mon, Ultimo, *move*,' shouted Lorenzo, who sensed my hesitation. His voice was hoarse with excitement, and as he shouted he kept firing wildly, without pause.

"A bullet sizzled a few centimetres from me, whistling shrilly as it passed my ear. I was now at the top of the hill, and we were nearly safe. We ran into the forest like maniacs, ripping our clothes on the thorns and prickles until we reached and crossed the Serchia River. We kept going, past another series of valleys filled with ancient battlements. In the distance we could see Castle Brolio, which the Nazis were employing as a headquarters, as well as the castles of Meleto, Tornano, Lecchi and Cacchiano.

"Those fields that as a child I had trod without a care, happy-go-lucky, were now the site of my flight for survival; I was prey to a pack of bloodthirsty hounds. I can't even guess how long we ran for our lives; it seemed hours. We swam across the Arbia River, and on its opposite bank pulled ourselves out, clawing into the mud, utterly without breath. Then we lurched through the dense vegetation of Monte Luco until we stumbled across a tumble-down barn.

"We plunged into its dark, dank interior and fell onto our backs, heaving and groaning. We were safe, by the merest whim of fate—our companions, to a man, had not been so lucky. All were now dead; and I still carried the flesh and blood of one on my clothing, as a reminder of what we had escaped."

Chapter 36

6ᵗʰ of October 1994 - Dawn

It was increasingly evident that we'd not be sleeping that night. The fire continued crackling in the dark, and we took turns tending it; we also opened another bottle of wine. From his jacket Ultimo produced an ancient, rusty tin, and handed it to me. On the lid was a dent from a bullet.

"See, *nini*, they say that smoking kills you; but if I hadn't had the habit, I'd have been dead a long time ago. This is the very tobacco tin I placed in my breast pocket the night before the ambush. That simple gesture of love for Elena—placing her image close to my heart—saved my life, for the tin took the bullet of a German sniper. Also, had I not tried to save Angelo by carrying him on my shoulders, I would have been killed as well; the poor boy acted as a shield for machine-gun fire, which he ended up taking instead of me. I was alive due to a series of unforeseeable quirks."

He said this with a wry smile as he stroked his three-day beard; his fingers ran across the white scar on his cheek, which glowed in the firelight. He was at peace with how fortunate he'd been, somehow surviving the massacres that took place in the days before the liberation. The war was coming to an end, but the population was made to suffer the final, homicidal retribution of the Nazi and Fascist forces. "Within just a few miles, in Scalvaia," Ultimo recalled, "the Guardia Nazionale Repubblicana executed sixteen partisans and civilians; in Monteriggioni, nineteen freedom fighters; in Cortona, the Nazis blew up a *podere,* killing ten *mezzadri*. In Civitella, the Herman Goering Division, following a clash with the par-

139

tisans where two German soldiers were killed, stormed into homes and even the church during mass, and took reprisals, slaughtering in just a few hours two hundred and forty-four people, mostly women and children.

"In Cavriglia, the same division massacred, without any provocation, a hundred and ninety-one workers as they were reaping wheat; in Padulivo di Vicchio, the German army murdered fifteen civilians; in San Polo, thirty-eight, as well as seventeen partisans; in Sant' Anna they exterminated five hundred and sixty persons—the entire village, and with such animal ferocity more than a third of the bodies were left unidentifiable.

"Bruno Bonci had been killed the day before our ambush in Vagliagli, where you live, *nini*. And let's not forget about the adjoining regions, where entire villages were swept away in fits of fury by the retreating German troops.

"That night, we found refuge right here, in this very edifice, as it was illuminated by the glare of antiaircraft cannon blasts in the sky. The British Spitfires attacked Castle Brolio, and everywhere in the valleys, explosions reverberated. After five hundred years of sweet peace, total war had reached the heart of Chianti and enveloped it in a blaze of death and terror."

Chapter 37

Ultimo's generous resolution

Finally, Ultimo decreed that the time had come time to rest, even as the first shafts of dawn were piercing the obscurity within the four stone walls surrounding us. We took a few hours' catnap in our tangled beds, and when the sunlight would no longer permit us to sleep—prying its way between our eyelids—we got up and rekindled the fire, bringing back an interior glow to compete with the exterior glare.

Ultimo continued his chronicles from exactly the point at which he'd left off a few hours before. "Lorenzo and I found refuge right here, where you and I are now, *nini;* but we had nothing to eat, and couldn't light a fire for fear of being discovered. All night long the bombardments continued, but in the morning all was silence. I was exhausted, curled up in a damp corner with my face pressed against soil that smelled of loam, musk and dew; a breeze brought with it the perfume of a nearby cypress.

"The logical thing to do now was to try to reach the Allied army, which should be just a few miles to the south. Before we departed, Lorenzo climbed a tree to see if he could spot any signs of movement. I waited in the barn for him to call out; but a few moments later he came scrambling down again, and waved for me to be silent. He raced back inside and in a low, panicked voice told me he'd seen a Nazi patrol headed in our direction, and that we were surrounded. Our chances of evading them were nil.

"I tried to remain calm, even as Lorenzo's terror prickled my skin; he had gone white as a sheet. Then I too caught sight of them through the window, and knew at once that this was an entire legion. It was clear that they were headed straight for the barn in search of partisans.

" 'Lorenzo,' I said, 'go and hide in the corner.'

"'Why? What do you have in mind, Ultimo?'

"'There's no sense in us both being taken. Just lie down and be still. I'm about to save your life. When the way is clear, go back to the *Macie* and take care of my family.' I corrected myself. *'Our* family. Elena included.'

"He did as I bid him, and went to that corner just there, where as you see there is a slight subsidence, and curled himself into the foetal position. I covered him with a few loose rocks…in fact, these right here, *nini."* He picked one up and displayed it to me, turning it over and over in his hands, like a precious artefact, before delicately replacing it in the exact spot from whence he'd taken it.

"Within a few minutes, I had completely buried him. All I could do now was go outside with my hands over my head, and surrender myself to my destiny. I stood there motionless, seized by a sudden sense of loss and a curious torpor. A young officer approached me, rifle drawn, shouting at me in a tongue I didn't know. He forced me to kneel, and several soldiers raced by us and into the barn. One of them returned moments later holding Lorenzo's leather jacket, which in the confusion I had forgotten to hide.

"He searched the pockets and found Lorenzo's Fascist Party membership card, and handed it over to his superior. The officer, whose excitement was manifesting itself in a particularly acrid body odour, regarded the document with bulging eyes. Then he took his leather glove and struck me across the face with it, and in stilted but comprehensible Italian, said, 'Lorenzo Terrosi, you are under arrest.' The young soldier next to him rammed the butt of his rifle into my face, knocking out my tooth and sending me to the ground, where I blacked out."

Here Ultimo paused and pulled back his lip to reveal the gap where the tooth had once been. "I came to inside a track-laying military vehicle," he said, "lying between two rows of seated soldiers. They seemed so young, so innocent; it was inconceivable to me that these red-cheeked teenagers were members of the infamous Hermann Goering division, responsible for the slaughter of entire villages of defenceless *Chiantigiani.*"

Chapter 38

10ᵗʰ of October 2008

I had drifted away from all trace of humanity and reached the sublimation of extreme solitude. It was a kind of bliss.

On I walked, assailed by a multitude of sweet, unfathomable reflections. At this point my destination was mere hours away. The only remaining obstacle was one more hill, and as I approached it my steps grew heavier due to the muck and mire through which I trudged. Fortunately, it had now stopped raining and the sun peered timidly from behind the retreating black clouds, its feeble radiance trickling through the bare branches of the forest and winking in the muddy puddles. The cry of a magpie rent the air, but the bird itself was hidden somewhere in the opalescent silvery boughs of a long untended olive grove.

As I said, bliss; yet what wouldn't I have given for some unexpected accommodation to spring into view, bringing with it the possibility of a shower and a shave and a hot meal. But I knew I would have to settle for bunking up in the old barn, in my soaked clothing, for another night—that is, if I were lucky. Possibly the whole thing had tumbled down by now, in which case I'd be left with no shelter at all.

Again I wondered why Ultimo had directed me there; what motivated him, on his deathbed, to send a lifelong friend away from him, into the rubble of his past. Could it just be so that I might read a letter that I could comfortably have read in my own living room? No, there must be a deeper reason, and I would surely discover it when I arrived.

In the meantime I must cherish the expectation. This was

certainly the most stimulating aspect of my journey: thinking about Ultimo, and recalling his life. During the course of ascending that final hill, I found myself once again hearing his voice, relating the most moving sequence in his long history…

Chapter 39

Fossoli

"The military transport on which I lay, face down on the metal grating, bounced along the loose country track. The callow soldiers on either side of me used my body as a boot rest, occasionally giving me a swift kick in my sides to keep me from squirming. My mouth was still seeping blood, which I was forced to swallow, and my injured jaw was swollen and tender.

"In a few hours we came to a halt. I was pulled from the vehicle and brusquely escorted into the *Carabinieri* station in the town of Poggibonsi, where I was locked in a small wooden cell. I turned and saw that I wasn't alone; squatting on a bench in the corner was another prisoner, and despite my vision still being blurred by my blow to the head, I recognized him instantly: Count Terrosi. He looked up with desolate eyes, and I saw how completely he had shed his once regal demeanour: he was unshaven and unkempt, his formerly sculpted moustache like a whisk broom, his clothing, which once reflected his magnificence, now threadbare and ill-fitting. He seemed physically diminished, a puny parody of his former self, weakened and withered. But at the sight of me recognition flashed in his eyes, momentarily recalling the man he had been.

"As soon as our jailers turned the key and left us alone, he addressed me in a voice both hushed and urgent: 'Ultimo, is that really you? What news of Lorenzo, is he safe?' And as he spoke he took from his back pocket a square of cloth with which I might clean myself of dried blood. It was a simple act, but it revealed to me how much the world had changed: the great Count Terrosi, pleading with me for news; offering me aid in my discomfort.

"I had difficulty speaking due to spasms of pain, but took a deep breath and managed to reply with pride: 'Lorenzo is safe! He evaded them.' To which the Count, the formidable figure of my youth, astonished me even further by sobbing like an infant.

"I sat beside him and brought him, albeit with many interruptions due to my pains, up to date on recent events, and above all explained why he must pretend to be my father, for to the best knowledge of our captors, *I* was Lorenzo. He then returned the favor, informing me that a German division had come to the village. Through Sandro, his factotum, he learned of their pillages and the terror they had been sowing among the people. He confirmed that the S.S. had blown up the medieval gate, and that Sante, my ancient enemy and the Count's former gardener, had come with a group of Fascist *squadristi* to the castle to arrest him in person.

"'What will become of us, Count?' I asked, not really expecting him to know. But he was better informed than I thought. He said:

"'Tomorrow we will be taken to Emilia, then on to a prison camp in Fossoli. After that, I have no idea." He sighed and looked very dejected; then turned to me and, with something of his old spirit, said, "I advise you to confess your true identity. You will fare better as Ultimo Gori than you would as my son. I have heard gruesome accounts of mass deportations of Jews to dreadful labor camps in Eastern Europe.'

"Thank you, Count, but I'm not certain I *would* fare better as Ultimo Gori, for I killed Eugenio Fanti, one of the Fascist chiefs in the village. If I revealed my true identity, it's most likely I'd be executed on the spot.'

"He looked at me with eyes haunted by guilt, and said, 'Ultimo, I beg your pardon for all of the suffering I have brought to our people. If I had only known what Fascism would degenerate into.' I gestured that he should go no further, as there was no sense in hearing those words now.

"'Don't speak of it, Count; let us instead hoard our strength. The war is almost over and we stand a fair chance of surviving. Until then, let's consign our souls to Providence and hope that sometime soon they bring us something to eat, so we can rest.'

"Some time later a soldier recalled our presence, and brought us a morsel of stale black bread and a bowl of water. Refreshed, we conversed deep into the night, lying on our hammocks without sheets, until fatigue overcame us, and we slept.

"We were awakened by the sound of Allied bombs falling all around Poggibonsi. An officer, sullen-faced, hard and hairy, came and barked a volley of commands at us, of which I only recognized *'Juden raus!'* Those words made me understand that I had, truly, assumed a new identity. From thenceforth, for all practical purposes, I was Jewish.

"Along with another group of desperates, which included two families with numerous children, we were taken to a train station and crammed into a dark, malodorous cabin used for transporting animals. As the Count had foretold, we were destined for Fossoli.

"The families, both Jewish, had been captured in Siena. They told us of how their home had been invaded by a command of Nazis led by the local Fascists, who gave them just a few minutes to pack up some essentials before leading them away to prison. Apparently, they had been just days away from liberation, for the city was now under Allied control and most likely liberation was imminent for Chianti as well.

As we spoke, the train lurched into motion. In a few hours we would reach our destination.

"Fossoli had been built in 1942 to hold English, Australian and New Zealand prisoners from the front in North Africa. It was then modified as a holding ground for prisoners in transit to the concentration camps of Buchenwald, Bergen-Belsen, Mauthausen, Ravensbrueck and mainly Auschwitz-Birkenau.

"The farther the train moved northwards, the fewer chances we had for rescue. I could sense my freedom slipping inexorably away at every station we passed.

"In the evening we reached Carpi in Emilia and were shifted to another coach that led us to the camp at Fossoli. It was a place of squalid brick barracks, all identical, inhabited by hundreds of internees, the vast majority of whom shared one offence: they were Jewish. The prisoners were not only Italian, but from as far away as Tunisia.

"The Count and I were housed together, and we remained nearly inseparable over the next several days. In truth we didn't have much to do when not exchanging information gleaned from the other inmates. The German guards watched us closely, and we quickly learned that it was best not to ask any questions and to obey blindly all of their orders. We were reasonably certain our stay would not be a long one, as no prisoner we questioned had been there more than a few weeks. We tried to calm our fears by telling ourselves that wherever we were sent would be no worse. If they wanted to kill us, why hold us here first? Why go to the trouble of transporting us elsewhere if they were only going to dispense with us when we arrived? Also, they fed us, didn't they? True, it was just pallid slop in rusty mess tins, but it was food. And we slept in bunk beds. It was survivable.

"We kept hoping for rescue; but this was difficult when

no news could make it past the barbed wire of our enclosure. Meantime, the Count and I continued to present ourselves as father and son. In fact, I became accustomed to calling him *babbo.*

"Then the day of our transfer arrived."

Chapter 40

Auschwitz - Birkenau

Ultimo's story had taken a turn I had never expected. He was fully engrossed in his narrative now; like an overflowing river, he brimmed with detail and description, in such a way that I could not but understand that this was the first time he had ever spoken of it to anyone. Hidden drawers of memory were opening, and I was coming to understand why he had so long kept them shut. "We may wear ourselves out trying," he said with surprising composure, "but no one can put such things as we saw then, into words. No one.

"One morning we were awakened by the bark of the warden, ordering us to collect our few belongings and prepare for relocation. I had nothing but the clothes on my back and some shirts Count Terrosi had given me. At the Carpi train station, we were boarded onto wagons used to transport cattle: men, women and children crammed like sardines, so many and so tightly that we had difficulty sitting on the wooden planks. The vast majority were Jews, but there were also some conscientious objectors and a few young partisans. There were just a few slender openings for air; the oxygen was thick and the heat unbearable.

"We took turns evacuating into a hole in the corner of the coach that opened directly onto the tracks below. Very soon the odor became excruciating. I was familiar with the scents of nature, having inhaled animal manure at the *Macie* my whole life, but the fetid stench of human waste is something you can never grow accustomed to. The children cried continually and the elderly bemoaned the lack of water. The nights were endless and cold, and we tried to sleep crouched against each other to share our body heat. I sought glimpses of the countryside through the slits, as the northern Italian plains of the Padana transformed into the Alpine mountains. The farther north we went, the less recognizable were the names of the stations. Then the train passed the Brennero border and we entered foreign lands completely unknown to me.

"We entered Czechoslovakia and then Poland. Every now and then the train would slow down and soldiers would toss us some stale bread, and we would launch ourselves onto it like a pack of beasts. Generally, though devoid of hope, we tried to retain our humanity and divide the morsels, granting precedence to the weakest.

"Finally, after I don't know how many days, the train came to a sudden halt. The hatch doors opened and we were signalled to come out. Some of us descended via the left platform, while others went to the right. I realized later that my companions who innocently chose the left were taken directly to the gas chambers. I myself was headed for that exit, but the Count grabbed my arm and directed me to his suitcase, which was on the opposite side of the cabin; and as a logical consequence we departed on the right side of the train instead.

"An impeccably uniformed S.S. guard ordered all of us to discard our suitcases; the Count was among the few who could comprehend German, and he conveyed this directive to the others. Then the men were separated from the women and children, and there was a flurry of panic. Fathers who tried to reunite with their families were beaten to death right then and there, so that all struggle quickly ceased.

"We were then ordered to pass before a corporal seated at a wooden table whose task it was to make a summary selection. The elderly and the children accompanied by their mothers were sent through a door to his left; others, victims of adversity like myself, were led to a corridor to his right. Once again, the right meant life; those who went the opposite way ended up under the death showers. I was separated from Count Terrosi here, and my last image of him is of his humbled, shaken countenance, his eyes holding fast to mine, as he said, 'Thank you, my son; take care of yourself, and of Lorenzo.' It was as if he were aware of what destiny awaited him.

"I was in Auschwitz, *nini*. By far the most horrifying of places ever created by man, comparable only to the most malignant circle of Dante's Inferno; the harrowing apex of human degeneracy.

"They stripped us of our clothes and sheared off our hair, and we were forced to wear striped uniforms with a yellow Star of David badge sewn onto the breast. Then, in an ultimate act of inhumanity, we were branded with a series of numbers; they were tattooed onto our left wrist.

"I was no longer human. I had mutated into a kind of spectre—a *Haftling,* as we were deplorably classified by our warders."

He lowered his gaze and then slowly rolled up his shirtsleeve, uncovering for the first time in my presence the six indelible numerals that he had always kept hidden from me. He stared at them, almost as though they were something separate from himself.

"As a farmer I was in robust health and was accustomed to performing manual labor. This put me in something of a privileged situation. In the barracks to which I was assigned there were mostly doctors, professors, and other professional sorts who had never had to experience sustained physical work. It was very hard on them, much more so than it was on me.

"But even I could not long endure the relentless brutality of our enforced duties. Just a few weeks were enough to render me a mere shade of my former self. I have no idea where I found the strength to adapt to those dreadful conditions. We were provided food only once a day—if 'food' is the proper word for the insipid liquid slop we were made to ingest, affording us only minimal subsistence. In the mornings, the *kapos,* or head guards, escorted us in columns of five to work in the fields, and there we remained until sunset, emaciating and dehydrating while at the same time being mocked and beaten relentlessly. Our captors were ruthless sadists, without an atom of humanity; devoid of pity or piety, purely visceral in their appetites.

"For many weeks I managed to hang on, breaking my back in those rocky fields, bounded on all sides by barbed wire. I was convinced that I had hit bottom, *nini,* but alas I was mistaken, as the worst was yet to come. A *kapo* who had taken a dislike to me for no apparent reason, ordered me to perform a far more terrifying task, and assigned me to the *Sonderkommando,* the *Kommando* in charge of the gas chambers and crematoriums. I was transferred to Birkenau, a few miles from Auschwitz, were the so-called 'final solution' took place.

"My chore was to collect the corpses from the gas chambers and transfer them to the crematorium ovens. My luckless associates and I piled up the skeletal bodies on the carts, well aware that all of those who were part of this *Kommando* would periodically be exterminated too. It was just a matter of time. This awful presentiment weighed so heavily on me that I lost the use of speech, and remained thus afflicted for the rest of my internment in that godforsaken place."

Ultimo fell silent. His expression had altered; his ruddy face was now nearly ashen, and the veins in his neck were swollen and throbbing. With nearly mechanical movements his hand went in search of a cigarette in his breast pocket; he placed it on his lower lip and lit it, then, after several gusts of smoke had somewhat restored him, he felt able to continue again.

"It took just a few weeks for me to become the senior member of the staff. It seemed the selections were occurring more frequently. Sometimes I recognized the corpses of my barracks companions among the heaps of cadavers; but it wasn't always easy to recognize them. In Auschwitz, we all became identical: bodies were mere skin and bone, our complexions were grey, our eyes hollow. Each of us had lost the distinguishing inner light that made us identifiably ourselves.

"When new inmates arrived, fraught with anxiety and assailing us with questions, I stood mute and immobile before them. Those are the faces that populate my nightmares to this day: their countenances devoid of any recognizable human feature, and yet still so desperate to cling to life. If I had to choose a single image to encapsulate the whole experience, it would be that. It is certainly the one most familiar to me: the line of gaunt faces, bowed heads, and bent shoulders, without thought, almost without sentience…but not without fear. When everything else that makes us human is gone, fear yet remains.

"There were prisoners from every corner of Europe, and the camp became a sort of Babel; people learned to communicate in Yiddish, which served as a kind of *lingua franca*. I of course persisted in my silence—I knew no Yiddish, knew no language but Italian and the basic French I had been taught by tutor Furini at Castello Susi—but I was also afraid to speak. I said nothing even as I watched young boys being selected to serve the paedophilic perversions of the S.S. elite, or the most attractive women being taken for official rape. I kept silent when the S.S. would launch screaming babies into the air and shoot them like clay pigeons. My eyes filled with rage as the guards reduced to bloody pulp those who committed the crime of approaching the barbed wire; but my lips were still. I kept mute when they stormed our barracks and pulled prisoners at random from our stunted beds, to serve as human guinea pigs in their deranged lab experiments. And I was mute during the eighteen hours each day I collected the lifeless corpses and with my bare hands disposed of them in the incinerators. I scrutinized the smoke that spiralled sluggishly from those baleful chimneys, dispersing ash as the wind directed; and sometimes the cinders would descend on me, the last, insubstantial traces of hundreds, thousands, perhaps millions of human beings whose guilt was to be Jewish, or Gypsies, or worshipers of Jehovah.

"Winter seemed suddenly to arrive and yet we remained in our lightweight uniforms, shivering in the ice, our ankles deep in snow that bit our feet; and our only respite was the filthy barracks, where we lay in our hundreds, infested with lice, mired in filth and desperation. Despite this, *nini*, I never shed a tear, not once. Somehow, I would always find something, some isolated, untouched place in my soul, in which there still shone a glimmer of hope.

"That hope was folly; an irrational belief that in spite of everything, I would one day be free to return to these hills, embrace my mother and my sisters, hold Elena's shining face in my hands. That I would once again enjoy shooting the breeze with Lorenzo, or even the gentle buffoonery of Armido and Adelmo. I kept these images of my previous life buried deep within me, so that at night, my dreams did not abandon me. Sometimes, in a half-awakened state, I could smell the boiling must in vats during the grape harvest; or the aroma of olives just crushed in the oil mills; the fragrant effluvium of lavender and rosemary bushes in summer; the liquorice exhalation of wild fennel. I would be taken by a whiff of wild garlic, or the musky pungency of wet earth following a storm in the fall; the stale sweetness of the cellars, the acrid bite of hay mixed with manure in the stables, the savory scent of the cypress forests in summer, and the sugary essence of the acacia and Spanish bloom flowers. And then the moment would pass and I would come to full wakefulness…and I would know instantly where I was. For in Auschwitz, there reigned but one ubiquitous odor: that of the dying and of death. You never grow accustomed to that, *nini,* especially in winter when the sky is perpetually low and oppressive, giving a sepulchral cast to all below it.

"And yet…somewhere it was written that I should elude death. I had avoided it by means of the tin tobacco box containing Elena's photo…and again when Angelo's body, slung over my shoulder, took machine-gun fire that would otherwise have riddled me…and again when Count Terrosi drew me away from the left side of the train so that I might carry his suitcase for him. And now again, at Birkenau, I was pulled from death's clutches by a fortuitous event.

"By January of 1945 I was myself a walking corpse of thirty kilos, forced to drag my near-lifeless limbs about the camp. My face had sunken into my skull, and my ash-colored skin was no more than a layer of parchment over my decalcified bones. One day I lost consciousness, collapsing on the icy ground of the camp. A particularly benevolent French *kapo* granted that I be sent to the infirmary; but I knew only too well that those who arrived there in my condition, were simply sent the next day to the gas showers. But there was nothing I could do; I was without strength, half-dead already; I could not lift a finger on my own behalf.

"To my very great surprise, things went rather differently for me. During the night a multitude of events took place. For several hours I heard gunshots and commotion from somewhere beyond the infirmary; bellows and shouts, sounds of engines starting and receding angrily into the distance. The following morning, by contrast, a pall of silence hung over the camp. Somehow I managed to get to my feet and make my way through the rows of beds occupied by hundreds of ailing inmates. There was no trace of the doctors, nor of the S.S.

"When I got to the door I saw that the camp had been abandoned. The officials had all evacuated, leaving the inmates dead on the ground, their faces rimmed with frost, the ground beneath them black with blood.

"We remained in the infirmary for four days in that surreal silence, occasionally going out to search for food left behind by the Nazis. The cold was arctic, well below zero, but we managed to organize ourselves and divide up essential chores to help us eke out some manner of survival. On the fifth day, while I was collecting some snow to melt into water, I heard the rumble of a tank, and turned in time to see it break through the gate—an imposing armoured vehicle with a red star painted on its side. The Soviets had arrived; our liberators. I was free.

"The war was over, and I was still alive, due to a series of flukes and accidents no one could possibly have foreseen. The irony was astonishing. For five months I was spared the gas chambers because I was healthy enough to work; that final night, I was spared because I fell sick. If I hadn't been ordered to the infirmary, I would have been shot like all the rest of my companions of the *Sonderkommando*."

Chapter 41

7th of October 1994

For the entire morning I remained motionless, listening to Ultimo with my legs crossed on the brick wall of the barnyard. We've all heard about the horrors of the holocaust, but only a privileged few have had a firsthand account from a survivor, and the effect was transfixing.

Furthermore, this was an account that had never been given to anyone else, and consequently, none of it had acquired the smoothness of a polished narrative; it had emerged in a manner as raw and as jagged as though it had happened yesterday.

After having told me that for the five months of his incarceration he hadn't shed a single tear, Ultimo was suddenly overwhelmed by emotion. He turned his face from mine, directing his gaze at some point in the lush valley below, and quietly wept. Instead of streaming down his face, the tears were caught in the stubble on his cheek and dispersed.

I would never have dreamed he was a survivor of the holocaust; and the irony is that no one ever could have known. In the register of those saved, he would be listed as Lorenzo Terrosi. It was almost unfathomable that the loving self-sacrifice he performed to save Lorenzo's life, could have consigned him to such a hideous punishment.

I didn't know what to do; I felt I ought to say something, or perhaps give him a comforting embrace. But I couldn't find words to stand against the magnitude of what he'd told me, and likewise a hug seemed puny and diminishing; so I remained still and silent. This was all I could offer him:

respect. It was the only means of acknowledging the tragedy of what he'd gone through: I would wait; I would listen; I would attend him while he purged the abyss of his soul by sharing these memories with me.

Then, with such slowness that he seemed to me moving underwater, he pulled his sleeve back down around his wrist, covering the numbers with which he'd been branded. As long as I'd known him, he'd always worn that sleeve buttoned, even when the other was rolled up around his biceps. Now I knew why. The tattoo was an inescapable reminder of a time when he'd been rendered all but subhuman. He'd been a victim, this man for whom freedom meant so much—he'd given himself bravely into the hands of those infected by madness, an ideology of death, an entire nation in the grips of unprecedented Mephistophelian bloodlust.

Ultimo soon regained his composure and became his usual self. He restarted the fire and filled up the pot with water, and almost as if wanting to exorcize his sufferings with the grace of the quotidian, he simply said, "How about some spaghetti with oil and garlic?"

Chapter 42

10th of October 2008

At long last I reached my goal. The old barn began to take shape in the distance. At first glance, it didn't appear to be as dilapidated a ruin as I recalled from my one and only visit, in Ultimo's company so many years prior. As I drew nearer I discerned that in fact the roof appeared in perfect shape, and the walls fortified.

Moreover, the yard had been cleared and even the trees were pruned; some of them even appeared freshly planted. The entire structure had, amazingly, been recently restored. Looking at it in bewildered awe, I recalled Ultimo's words: "Often, *nini,* while contemplating this eternal view, I have let my imagination go, and fantasized making this the site of my own personal *osteria.*"

The walls had been repaired with care, the cracks stuccoed, the roof laid with new-fangled terracotta tiles, and the windows fitted with new panes and frames. The pergola was covered with wattle surmounted by flourishing jasmine that shaded the yard, about which were placed tables and chairs. There were also some pots filled with withering flowers that had been visibly tended until they were in season.

To say that I was staggered is inadequate. I could scarcely recognize the wreck to which Ultimo had brought me a quarter-century before. Ultimo had obviously spent a tremendous amount of time and energy reconstructing the place to match his vision, all the while keeping it secret from me. I found myself recalling something else he'd said—though I couldn't mark the occasion: "When two people share a secret, it's a secret no longer."

I sat on the arm of a chair by the restored well and extracted from my knapsack the key Ultimo had given me, along with the envelope. I held them for a while, lost in thought, contemplating the results of Ultimo's zeal and artistry with enchantment and approval.

Having examined the exterior, it was time to enter. The door had been repaired and varnished, and Ultimo had also reinstalled the original lock, cleared of rust and well lubricated. I inserted the key and gave it a twist; just a flick of the wrist and the door glided open, with no squeals of protest.

As surprised as I was by the changes to the exterior, the interior was, if possible, even more extraordinary. I found myself in an ample welcoming hall with whitewashed walls—excepting one which retained the original raw stone, on which hung ancient tools that had once belonged to local peasants. The floor had been sandblasted, revealing the original wide granite slabs, worn smooth over the course of many years.

The room was filled with oak chairs and tables that needed only to be set for dinner. On the opposite side of the room was a cherry wood counter that functioned as a bar, and extended from a wall from which also hung a plate rack and shelves filled with unlabeled straw flasks and clay-colored cups. On the counter rested a knife block sheathing a collection of blades of all sizes. The fireplace had been entirely rebuilt utilizing the original cypress beam that had been cleansed of woodworms, and the hearth was now wide enough to contain a bench on each side.

In the corner of the room were two staircases: one ascending, the other leading to the cellar. I decided to explore the upper level first, and climbed the artisan-made steps, neatly stroked with a plane and varnished. I emerged in a tiny attic with a wooden floor on which rested a comfortable bed with two pillows. On one side was a bedside table with a marble surface, atop which was a bronze candlestick with a scarlet candle that had never yet been lit. There was also a ceramic basin and a mirror, and I looked at myself for the first time in three days: my face unshaven, my skin dry and dingy, my long hair matted and stringy.

I gave in to a sudden urge to test the firmness of the mattress by pressing it with my palm; it felt soft and pliable, inviting me to rest. I stretched out across it, and from that comfortable perspective I was able to appreciate the ceiling, crossed by small chestnut beams alternating with crimson bricks.

He had left nothing overlooked; the entire property had been painstakingly restored to the smallest detail.

I sprang up and went back to the staircase, and descended into the cellar, which had been dug out of bare earth. There was no light, so I struck a match and lit a petrol lamp placed close to the entrance.

On the ceiling hung salamis and hams, releasing a brackish perfume; the ground was covered by small pebbles that stuck in the soles of my amphibious boots; and two large demijohns stood tall on the floor, like sentries.

Ultimo had surprised me yet again; it was apparent that he had worked on this place for years, tirelessly turning a crumbling ruin into a jewel—a jewel mounted like a gem in the heart of Chianti. I tried to comprehend how he transported the tools and materials required, to this remote location. Certainly there was no running water or electricity; but he had installed a small bathroom at the rear with a draining channel that led down into the depths of the ground. All I needed to do was fill up a pot with the well water, light the fire, have a wash and a shave, and cook a plate of pasta.

Then, the time was ripe to read the letter.

Chapter 43

6th of October 1994

A falling stillness prevailed on that October day. The usual cascade of waning light caused me to blink in the evening splendor as I followed Ultimo into the woods to collect chestnuts, and to wash our plates and pans and fill our bottles in the gurgling spring. Later, armed with threads and hooks, we went to the creek to fish for trout. We scraped the soil to unearth maggots to use as bait; then, when our lines were in the crystal-clear water and we were awaiting our first nibbles, Ultimo recounted what had transpired in the days following his liberation.

"What immediately followed the arrival of the Russians, remains a blur; I don't recall even how many more days we spent at Auschwitz. Hours, minutes, even seconds had long since lost all relevance to me; I'd survived those months with only one motive in mind: to make it through to the end of the day alive. Each day that went by represented one day closer to a hypothetical freedom—or to my ignoble end. Long life was granted to no one, in a concentration camp; we were like food stamped with an expiration date; once we reached it, we were removed, discarded, swept from the shelf into the dustbin.

"Even after our liberators had arrived and my freedom was certain, I remained stuck in this mode; though gradually we all began to feel the change. We were once again locked up in our barracks, but there were far fewer of us now; and thus, with empty beds, we could use as many blankets as we wished.

"The Russians limited their interaction with us to providing us meals; otherwise they merely looked at us with eyes that hid none of their pity. I could not imagine how we must appear to them, but I was grateful they respected our suffering.

"As the days passed, with adequate sleep and nutrition and no more stress or hard labor, I slowly became more recognizably human. My hair grew back; I gained a little weight. But my faculty of speech did not return. I remained mute as an animal.

"After a few weeks, we were finally informed that we would be transferred and, once again, I was on a train—though this time, not in cargo, but in a passenger car; I felt that I had in some small way rejoined the human race. We were conducted to a refugee camp in Hungary, where conditions were tough and hygiene spotty. Still, we weren't prisoners and were not required to work, which was a blessing; our tormented bodies would not have been able to sustain any further abuse. All that was required of us was that we keep the barracks clean and respect the rules and schedules.

"The few countrymen present, most of whom were from northern Italy, were assigned to the same barracks. One young man was called Constantino; he was still a teenager, almost twenty years my junior. He slept on the bunk bed above me and was extremely informative. He told me he'd been captured in the province of Verona while fighting as a partisan, and had been interned as a political prisoner. He hadn't experienced the horrors of Auschwitz, but had been imprisoned in a site under the Luftwaffe's control that by comparison to what I had endured sounded like a sort of holiday camp. He was extremely jovial and we established a friendly rapport. It was thanks to him that I regained my powers of speech, and also, more gradually, a nascent sense of optimism.

"Eventually I told him my entire story and also revealed my true identity. As I said, I can't remember how much time had passed; but we are definitely talking months. And shortly thereafter, Germany finally surrendered, and the much yearned-for day of freedom finally arrived. I was granted a rail pass to Italy, to Tuscany, to Chianti, to my beloved *Macie.*

"We travelled the first part of the journey together, Constantino and I, until our paths diverged; and I have never seen nor heard from him since." At this point in the story something tugged on Ultimo's fishing line, and he paused to reel in a plump, wiggling trout. When he had removed it from the hook and had his line again in the water, he picked up where he had left off.

"Many rail tracks had been blocked. Wherever my gaze fell, there were signs of war: rubble, debris, even human remains. After a few weeks of begging for food, or working in exchange for a plate of soup or piece of bread in the cities where the train would stop, my journey came to an end. We crossed the Swiss border into Italy, and eventually came to the Siena train station.

"Immediately I set off on foot toward the Chianti hills. Seeing those landscapes again swelled my heart; treading that familiar soil, breathing in the scents of my cherished countryside, gave me a palpable feeling of affirmation, even triumph.

"Lifting my gaze to the sky, toward those familiar vaults, I felt myself saturated by the radiant splendor of all the elements surrounding me. Those wide expanses of land and sky tasted of liberty, to me. I felt like the prodigal son in the biblical parable.

"But when I caught my first glimpse of my village, perched atop the hill, I was unexpectedly cast into the deepest melancholy, and an uneasy shiver ran down my spine. The medieval gate was no longer there. That imposing entrance, which for centuries had greeted visitors in peacetime and thwarted invaders in wartime, had been blown up, as had many other buildings now deleted from the landscape.

"Still, the village itself had survived; as I entered I saw commercial activities taking place—the drugstore, the ironmonger, and the carpenter were fully engaged in their trades. I passed many familiar faces, but it became quickly obvious that no one recognized me, and I had too many things on my mind to stop and greet them. All I desired was to find Elena. I even spotted Poppo, now without his Fascist uniform; he had returned to his post as the barber's apprentice.

"At the end of the main street, where it opens up onto the square, I saw in the distance the massive bulk of Don Mauro in his black cassock and three-cornered hat, so characteristic of country priests. He was conversing with a group of women. I approached him, and when I was within reach I placed the palm of my hand on his thick shoulder.

"'Don Mauro,' I said, interrupting his conversation. He turned slowly towards me, and gave me an inquisitive look.

"'I am Ultimo Gori,' I said. At the sound of my name the women covered their mouths and gasped in stupefaction. Don Mauro took me into a mighty, bearlike embrace; then asked me to go with him, he would cook me a hot meal."

Chapter 44

7ᵗʰ of October 1994

We prepared for another night at the bivouac, this time exchanging roles. Ultimo was now in charge of keeping the fire going and I took care of cooking the trout we'd caught earlier, which I gutted and stuffed with minced garlic and rosemary.

It had taken only a few days to learn the history of Ultimo's victimization in its entirety; I was missing only the epilogue, and I was certain that he was saving it for when we opened a bottle of wine.

The evening wasn't as cool as the previous night had been; the wind was now blowing from the south, bringing humidity in on its back. Still, the warmth of the fire was welcome, and when the first were sufficiently bronzed I drew them out of the skewers and pulled the cork from the bottle. As I'd guessed, the noise of the stopper being removed was for Ultimo a prompt.

"*Nini*, after having survived the concentration camp I was certain I would no longer need to embolden myself against fresh horrors. My miraculous escape from every peril had to have some final reward, some justification. And the only one I desired—the one which kept me going during those infernal days—was the possibility of once again embracing my loved ones. Now I was so close, everything in me wished to race straight to the *Macie;* but my respect for Don Mauro held me in his hospitality.

"He invited me into his humble parish house and ordered his maid to prepare me a heaping plate of *pappardelle,* and poured me a glass of wine in the meantime. It was my first taste of the fruits of my land in many, many months, and as that delicious nectar trickled down my throat, its warmth and mildness restored to me a sense of ease and comfort. When the meal arrived, its aroma was so rapturous that I began to consume it like a starving dog; but Don Mauro advised me to calm myself and savor the repast; afterwards we would discuss 'important matters.' Perhaps I was too giddy from the food and wine to have heard the emphasis he put on those words. Anyway, he said he would then escort me back to the *Macie,* if I wished.

"When I had eaten my fill, Don Mauro insisted I sit on his couch while he sat before me on a wooden chair. He lit a Tuscan cigar, took a deep breath as though making certain he had chosen the most fitting words, and commenced:

"'Ultimo, you are an extraordinary man. It's evident from your appearance that you have suffered much these many years. Now you must again be brave, as I must share with you the recent chronicle of your family, to the extent that I know it; I am alas not privy to every detail.

"'Let me begin by saying that the entire village was convinced you had died; in fact the local council added your name to the list of locals to be engraved on the monument erected in honor of the victims of the war.' He paused, stroked his pitch-black goatee, then set his smouldering cigar on the rim of the tin ashtray.

"'Then Lorenzo suddenly appeared at my door, informing me of your capture and how you had courageously given up yourself to save him—and what you asked of him in return. At that time the Nazis were swiftly retreating in an effort to avoid engagement with the Allies. But they chose to vent their anger before they departed. In the village, they shot ten people in retribution, among them Elena's mother, Isolina.'

"A shudder ran through me as I heard this, but he held his hand as if to forestall my next question, and added, 'Elena herself was not harmed.

"'Regrettably, Ultimo, the homicidal fury in the village did not appease the Nazis, nor did it spare your relatives. Sante led the German troops to the *Macie* to search for you after the *squadristi* discovered Eugenio Fanti's corpse by the river. I am sorry, my friend: they exterminated your family.'

"Don Mauro's voice was steady and composed, and he kept his eyes fixed on mine; it was as though he were suspending me in his narrative, lest I otherwise fall to pieces.

"'As I said, I don't know the specifics. Only Sante did, but he won't be able to reveal them as he was captured by the partisans and hung in the public square in Castellina in Chianti, before a large, jeering crowd that had tried to lynch him themselves, prior to the execution.'

"I listened, tightening my fists in rage and apprehension. I was so choked by emotion that I could only manage a few feeble syllables: 'All…of them? *All?*' To which Don Mauro sighed and nodded his massive head. Mamma, Giuseppina, Carlotta, Adelmo and Armido were no longer of this earth. They did not await me at the *Macie,* to ease my months of torment with the balm of their sweet affection.

"I was immobile, my mind a confusion; I lacked the will to act. My only sensation was numbness. Finally I asked what had happened to Lorenzo and Elena. Don Mauro shrugged. 'I know only this: In the days following the liberation Lorenzo came to tell me he was leaving. He was sailing from the port of Livorno for America. He asked me, if by some miracle you survived, to tell you that the *Macie* was yours: the Terrosi family would no more hold claim over it. The documents to this effect are deposited at the notary office in the village; you may collect them whenever you wish. And do not worry, Ultimo, *Notaio* Fanti doesn't despise you: he is well aware of the crimes committed by his son.'

"He then realized he might have said something inappropriate, as the last of my thoughts were obviously etched boldly on my face. 'What about Elena?' I asked, hoping for a more encouraging response, yet fearing the opposite.

"'She departed with Lorenzo,' he said. I felt the world drop out from beneath me; I was set adrift in a hostile cosmos. I could not rise from the couch; even the act of thinking was agony. I refilled the glass and drank, helping myself to more of the priests' wine; my hand trembled as I brought the glass to my lips, and I spilled scarlet droplets onto his rug.

"When I had finished the bottle Don Mauro stood up. 'Come,' he said, 'I will escort you in my calash.' And so I returned to the *Macie,* now empty of life, and I regretted, *nini,* I honestly regretted not having perished myself, that I might have been spared such agony. When Don Mauro left me, standing on the threshold not knowing how to find the courage to go in and face those vacant walls, he said, 'Have faith in God, Ultimo,' and he embraced me.

"I pushed him aside and snarled, 'God is dead to me, Don Mauro. Dead!' And I went in.

"So that is my story, *nini.* I have nothing more to tell you. The war swept away so many millions across the world, and among them everyone I ever loved. I wished to bring you here, as this was the place where I was captured, and where I saw Lorenzo for the very last time. He to whom I gave salvation, and in exchange he stole Elena from me.

"Let's try to get some rest now, as tomorrow at dawn we will depart." I tried to do as he said; but couldn't sleep because, as the crackle of the flames subsided, they were replaced by the muffled sounds of Ultimo sobbing. He lay with his back to me; and as I could think of no conceivable comfort I might give him, I let him be. Eventually, sleep drew me away.

Chapter 45

10th of October 2008

Ultimo's story, as I knew it, ended in the fall of 1945, with his return to the *Macie*. He had not told me how he lived afterward, nor had he ever divulged the contents of the letter that had so upset him when I first delivered it to him, all those years before. Now that very letter was resting right here on the mantelpiece, in its original envelope; all I had to do was open it. Ultimo had told me I should, at an opportune moment. I was cosily settled in the restored barn, with the fire blazing. I'd hung my soaked shirt and jeans before the hearth, using the chairs as a clotheshorse. I had bathed, shaved, and rested. I could not imagine any moment more opportune than this one.

With much trepidation, I removed the document and unfolded it; the paper was crinkled and yellowed with age. It was covered with script from a fountain pen, the handwriting neat and attractive. I filled a glass with red wine but decided not to sit; instead, with a candle in one hand and the letter in the other, I walked about the room reading the contents aloud.

San Francisco, Fall 1984
Dear Ultimo,
I've chosen to put pen to paper and write to you on this date, because exactly forty years have passed since our paths were so brutally divided. The final image I have of you is exceptionally vivid: you looming over me, lowering into place the very last stone that would essentially bury me alive, and spare me being

arrested and taken away to near-certain death. That stone obscured my sight, and cast me into a darkness from which I felt I might not ever emerge. My heart thumped like a hammer as the soldiers searched the area around my hiding place, so much so that I feared they might hear it and discover me. But before they could do so, one of them called out in excitement, and the others all ran to him. I realized that they had found my jacket; after which they exited the house, and soon thereafter I heard the sound of an engine receding in the distance.

I remained hidden beneath the rocks for another few hours, prey to hideous anxiety; and when at last I could endure it no more, I attempted to free myself. You had done your work very well, Ultimo; I was so thoroughly entombed that it took all my effort to dislodge the stones that pinioned me. At one point I feared I might be unable, and that I had cheated one death only by means of choosing another.

Once I had freed myself, I might have journeyed a few hundred yards south and reached the Allied army. I could actually make them out in the distance; it would have been so easy. But your words burned in my mind: you had charged me to look after your family—our family—and that was a debt of honor.

I surmised that you had allowed yourself to be mistaken for me; had you not, the Fascists would have certainly killed you. And yet I had heard from my father of the mass deportations of Jews to dreadful internment camps in Eastern Europe; were you to be sent there, as seemed likely, your survival seemed equally unlikely.

I returned to the village, arriving the following day. I was startled by the sight of a massive feast taking place; the villagers had flooded the streets and were dancing and drinking, celebrating the Nazi retreat. I made my way through the joyous crowds in search of Elena. I found her at her house, disconsolate because her mother *had been shot a few days before, along with nine other civilians, lined up against the Town Hall like criminals. I tried to calm her, but could only add to her woe when I told her of your arrest. But when I added that it was your wish that I conduct her to the Macie, she agreed.*

Again I made my way through the cavorting crowds, this time leading Elena by the hand. We passed through the square, where a huge bonfire had been lit and a local band was playing merry tunes. We ignored the celebrations, as for us that war seemed far from over; instead we trekked across the fields and woods until we came at last to the podere.

We found it languishing beneath an unnerving quiet. All we could hear were the bleats and cries of hungry animals from the stables. Then, in the dimming light, we made out the shapes of the bodies—the sad remains of the Gori family, strewn across the yard. It seemed obvious that they had been dragged from the house, lined up against the hay barn, and shot. I cautioned Elena to stay back as I examined them; they had all been pierced by a multitude of bullets, and lay motionless over blood-soaked dust.

The hands of your mother, Annita, were joined as if in a final beseeching prayer. Pina, in a valedictory gesture of merciful affection, embraced poor Carlotta. Armido and Adelmo's unseeing eyes were turned towards the stars, though terror was etched on their faces.

I shall never be able to banish these images from my mind; how could I? Even if I possessed the capacity to do so, I wouldn't; it is my duty to bear them, to carry them with me always, in tribute to your fallen family.

Ultimo, I am compelled to reveal to you many things that might yet, after all these years, afford you understanding and assuage your pain and suffering. I beg you to recognize that I suf-

fered too, having lost not only my adopted family, but something even more precious: Giuseppina, my sweet Pina l'Etrusca, was two months pregnant when those depraved bastards slew here. We had kept it secret, wishing to reveal it on the day the war was declared at an end, in order to add to the joy of the occasion; after which we would be married. Pina and I took such pleasure in imagining the surprise on your mother's face when she learned that she would soon be a nonna; and I took great joy in knowing that my extraordinary bond with you would be even more deeply sealed. But alas, it was not to be.

For Elena, to be facing this massacre so soon after having seen her mother murdered, and with no news of the fate of her brother or of you, the blow was debilitating. She collapsed in my arms. I carried her into the house and tended her there. I can assure you, Ultimo, passing the night in the deserted Macie, ringed by the bodies of its slain inhabitants, was an experience I would never wish to repeat.

Over the following days I organized the funerals of your mother, your sisters, and the twins. It seemed increasingly certain that you would never return, and thus the only remaining link between us was Elena. It may seem illogical, Ultimo, but it was for this reason that I asked her, almost on impulse, to come away with me and build a new life together elsewhere. We didn't love each other; she loved you, and I loved Pina. But we clung to each other to keep that love alive; it was our way of honoring you.

We needed to get as far away as possible from the place that was now filled only with ghosts; to stay there would ultimately have asphyxiated us. The means to escape came when I made the acquaintance of an Italian-American official named Todd Iacovone, who was put in temporary charge of the village. In exchange for Castello Susi, which had been the property of my family for centuries, he arranged for us travelling papers, a house, and even *a job in America. And while such an exchange may appear less than equitable, Elena and I accepted it without hesitation, and embarked on the next ship.*

We ended up in San Francisco, where months later a baby girl arrived. We decided, not by chance, to call her Vittoria. She is beyond doubt your daughter, Ultimo; she shares your temperament, your facial expressions, your reasoning, your curiosity, and above all your strength and generosity. She blossomed like a luxuriant Chianti grapevine, splendid and vigorous. She has lively eyes, the same turquoise as yours, and bringing her up has been a joy, so much compensation for so much suffering.

Vittoria is our only child; we had no more of our own, nor have we ever returned to Italy. I worked for many years for a firm that imports wines and spirits from all over the world, and each time I came across a flask of Chianti my mind would flash back to my childhood, when we played together without care within the castle walls; and it seemed incredible to me that I was ever that child, that I ever lived that life.

Many times I found myself travelling around the world, and each time I spotted that simple flask—even if it were empty and used as a candle-holder in a smoky bistro—I would feel, in a sense, at home; that I was not a stranger in a strange land, but that I had stumbled upon at a kind of spiritual Macie with the Gori family around me, and the antics of Armido and Adelmo filling the room.

A while ago I happened to make a business acquaintance with a merchant from Veneto, from whom we purchased wines produced in the Soave area. He was a pleasant fellow named Costantino Berton. We became good friends during his stay in America, and when I presented him with my card, bearing my full name, he suddenly turned pale. When I asked him what was wrong, he said that he had, in a sense, met me before. And then he told me the circumstances under which you and he came together in the refugee camp after the war, and how you had spoken of your many hardships and injustices, and how you even then were registered under the name of your lifelong friend, Count Lorenzo Terrosi.

I was stunned to hear that you had, against all the odds, survived; but my joy was muted by a sudden sense of guilt. I had taken Elena away, and with her, your last chance at restoring your life. I spent years trying to determine how best to write to you and explain my reasons; eventually I wrote to Don Mauro instead, hoping to hear from him that you had begun a new life built on the ashes of the old. But he informed me that you lived alone, like a hermit. I felt—I still feel—so negligent and ashamed, Ultimo. Especially because my marriage to Elena had by this time softened into a love match. Then three years ago, she passed away.

I revealed to Vittoria that her natural father was alive, and I told her all about you; but for some reason she decided not to seek you out. She is like you in that way, my friend; sometimes her decisions are a mystery to all around her. She now lives in Africa with her husband, Frank, providing aid to communities afflicted by famine, and I rarely hear from her. But she has a daughter, Annita, like her grandmother; and this girl—our granddaughter, Ultimo—is very keen to visit Italy, so much so that I left her a small apartment in the village; one of the few Terrosi properties I chose to keep. I expect that you will meet her soon, whether you are willing or no; she is unlikely to be put off, having inherited your stubbornness.

I have with great assiduity dreamed about you, Ultimo, and often consider returning to see you, for you have been the one true friend in all my life, and because your sacrifice has made possible all the joy I found afterwards. Often, before falling asleep,

I try to conjure you out of the darkness, working in the fields with that dreamy look of yours; or I imagine you, solitary in the woods, frequenting those places you know better than anyone alive, and which you love with such purity and ardor. Perhaps you have even returned to that barn in the Chianti hills where you so valiantly saved my life. Strangely, I discovered, after making many inquiries, that that barn has always belonged to my family; it bears the name, probably not by chance, of La Speranza: "hope", the greatest of all your gifts to me. In return I give La Speranza to you, though I don't know what its condition may be; possibly by now it is no more than rubble.

I have not yet decided in what manner I will direct this letter, and the key to the property, into your hands; I do not know that I have the courage to do so in person. I don't presume to ask for your forgiveness, and I require no response to this letter; you owe me nothing. I, on the other hand, owe you everything; after having taken so much from you. My only desire now is to repay you by whatever means I can. I hope it is not too little, too late.

I conclude this letter with one final revelation that perhaps it would be kinder to take to my grave; but I feel obliged to tell you, since I dare not withhold anything else from you, even though it seems likely to cause you even more distress. You will remember, Ultimo, the gossip in town that your brother, Primo, was actually my father's son; that is false. The last time I saw my father, he told me so personally. However, he admitted that there was a child born from his despotic relations with your mother: You.

Your blood brother,
Conte Lorenzo Terrosi

Chapter 46

10th of October 2008

I gently refolded the letter, slipped it back into the envelope, and returned it to the mantelpiece. Then I sat cross-legged on the straw mat that covered the granite floor before the fireplace and contemplated the flames. I savored the wine, taking small sips, running it over my taste buds to appreciate better its organoleptic qualities.

The chimney was sucking the smoke up the flue with vigor, consuming too greedily the logs I'd gathered for it. The candle had now gone out, so this was my only source of light, and the fire, perhaps sensing its sovereignty, made all the shadows dance in celebration, brightening the room with sensuous ripples.

And in this state of repose I turned my mind to Lorenzo. I thought back on my first meeting with him, when he'd given me the letter; I could still recall his features, his courteous and gentlemanlike manner and his articulate, cadenced speech. I had never asked Ultimo what sentiments he had for this man, who I now knew to be his brother; but I recalled his violent reaction when I delivered the letter to him a quarter-century ago. For the forty years prior to that he'd lived with a perfectly understandable resentment and grief; all he knew was that Lorenzo had left Italy with Elena, apparently leaving his family behind to be slaughtered.

I couldn't know for certain what Ultimo felt, of course; but it seemed to me that some of his anger and grief must have been assuaged by Lorenzo's letter. Lorenzo had, it seemed to me, acted honourably; he did not, after all, seize the chance to flee to the Allies and save himself, but had risked remaining in dangerous territory, still under nominal Nazi-Fascist control, to honor Ultimo's request.

He'd gone directly to the village in search of Elena, which he found free of occupying forces, though at a bloody price; and then on to the *Macie,* which was, alas, the same. Can we blame him for having arrived hours too late?...And if he had arrived earlier, before the massacre, what could he have done to prevent it? Was he even armed? And if he were, what could one rifle do against the fury of Sante and his entire division of bloodthirsty butchers? Surely his name, as well as Elena's, would have been added to the long list of victims of the war, and Ultimo would have blamed Lorenzo for taking Elena to the *Macie,* and cursed him for it for the rest of his life. Certainly the news of their departure together must have felt like a knife in his back, especially after his months of unspeakable suffering in the concentration camp, but what better alternative could there have been...?

From the letter it appears that it had been Elena's choice to embark with Lorenzo, given her belief that Ultimo was dead. We must also consider that she may, in the confusion of events and emotions, have subconsciously blamed Ultimo for her mother's death, since the reprisal was triggered by the discovery of Eugenio Fanti's body. And finally, would not Ultimo be contented to know that the man whose life he had saved was joined for life by the woman he had loved? Would he not have blessed a union between the two people he loved most, one of whom now carried in her womb the fruit of that love? Taking all of this into consideration, I could not but be convinced that once Ultimo read the letter he had not only forgiven Lorenzo, but had rehabilitated him in his mind, rediscovering the friend he believed he'd lost; and the fact that they were now revealed as sons of the same father perhaps nudged forgiveness into outright felicity.

If there was someone I felt sure I knew deeply, that person was undoubtedly Ultimo; and the only upset and irritation he displayed had been *before* I delivered the letter to him. During all the succeeding years, he never displayed that annoyance again. On the contrary, his behavior could be described as almost serene, a perfect acceptance of his life and himself. True, he was never sociable with anyone but me, and lived his life in almost total isolation from the world, with no television, radio or phone, and without ever moving outside the borders of Chianti. He never frequented the local bar, didn't possess a car or other mechanized means of transport, and as an atheist belonged to no congregation.

Yet he never had a bad word for anyone; he loved these hills and had completely invested himself in this territory. He possessed confidence and composure, and was proudly self-sufficient, raising hens, chickens, and rabbits; he also hunted. He cultivated vegetables and fruits, and tended the vineyard, producing from it a fine wine of which he made abundant use, as well as an exquisite olive oil.

He passed his spare time consulting books from the Terrosi library, left to him, along with the *Macie* by Lorenzo's bequest, and he had developed unbounded knowledge. But it wasn't just that he *knew* Chianti; I remembered vividly Lorenzo saying, when I asked who Ultimo was, "He is Chianti!" An eloquent response, summoning up in three words the essence of this extraordinary man.

Following our journey to the barn, I saw less of him; not because I lost interest in him, but in deference to his desire that I should live my own life and start a family—something I hadn't done. He permitted me one monthly visit, and often when I came to the *podere,* he wasn't there. Now it was evident where he had been all those times: here, reconstructing this very barn.

The most astonishing thing about him was that he seemed never to age. His mind remained nimble and quick; his body had endured only slight decline. His posture remained erect, his eyes were quick and clear, and his Herculean strength was undiminished. It was difficult for me to remember I was dealing with a man who a few months prior had passed the hundred-year mark. In celebration of which the mayor organized a feast in his honor, with live music, and even sent a car to pick him up; but Ultimo was nowhere to be found. He simply didn't believe he had accomplished anything out of the ordinary by merely rising each day after the next, so on the occasion of his centenary he walked ten miles alone, to bathe in the hot springs that gushed and gurgled in an oak wood.

I felt pleasantly exhausted by my long day, and from the effort of sorting through the events of Ultimo's life; and so I climbed up into the loft and into the bed. As I lay there, I considered two final questions: first, whether Ultimo regretted that Lorenzo hadn't delivered his letter in person, and second, whether Lorenzo now regretted it as well. Then it occurred to me to wonder: had Ultimo ever replied? Perhaps one day I would learn the answer. As I drifted off to sleep, it seemed abundantly clear there would be stories yet to come about Ultimo Gori.

Chapter 47

8th – *9th of October 1994*

Ultimo seemed to have been relieved of a burden. Following the revelation of his uncanny history, he was if possible more energetic, more unbridled. The days unravelled languidly as we retraced our original path, crossing the woods in the company of a sapphire sky and a fulgent sun; it was cold but dry. At one point he stopped to pick up a viper that crossed our paths; the poisonous creature appeared perfectly at ease with him, and wrapped itself around his arm. He pampered it for a bit, then kissed its triangular head and lowered it back to the rocky surface. I was glad to see him once again light-hearted; he seemed like a tree trunk floating on a current: massive, but graceful and swift.

Ultimo suggested we stop for the night by some hot springs. There we shed our clothes and, naked as worms, reclined in the naturally formed tubs, beneath layers of steaming calcareous deposits. Above us a canopy of stars whirled and sparkled. Ultimo wadded some mud between his palms, and when he had rendered it perfectly spherical he turned and flung it into my face, then laughed boyishly. I retaliated, and we passed a good portion of the night in mock combat, taunting each other and howling gleefully like children.

He then spoke of the years after the war, which were uneventful for him. After the unspeakable tragedies he had endured, it was a kind of relief to fall into a steady, unyielding rhythm—a changeless routine. As the new master of the *podere* he made a few innovations, such as replacing the oxen with a tractor, using the animals only to pull his cart. Working from dawn to dusk, with no help, he produced enough to live on; and if he had extra crops, he sold them to the local *Consorzio Agrario.*

He witnessed the population's flight from the impoverished countryside for the newly industrialized towns and cities. He lived firsthand the transfiguration of Chianti into a monoculture based almost exclusively on vineyards. He never considered leaving the *Macie,* not even when he received numerous proposals to purchase it, for substantial sums, from prosperous wineries that desired the land. Similarly, when tourism exploded in the area, he turned down offers from pompous foreign millionaires, eager to boast at their golf club that they were the owners of a holiday home in rural Tuscany.

His reclusive lifestyle sustained him in total fusion with the territory, and fostered in him a myriad of talents that he casually discovered and developed over time. Despite being a hunter, he established an intimate rapport with wildlife; animals felt comfortable approaching him, as they had done with his sister Carlotta. When he walked in the woods, he would attract a literal following: bucks, badgers, boars, foxes, porcupines and others would emerge from the underbrush and trot or trundle after him. However, when he hunted, this did not occur; then, the animals who otherwise found him so attractive kept hidden from him, even if he only sought squabs and pheasants.

Later, and by chance, he came to recognize his healing capacities. Placing his hand over a wound that he had received while cutting the grass with a sickle, he felt a warm tingle emanate from his palm and diffuse through his body; after which the wound seemed to knit itself up. He also discovered that he was a water diviner; he needed only to wield a Y-shaped twig or branch, and when he carried it over a vein of water the stems would faintly quiver. This is how he came to drill a well close to his Sangiovese vine, where he planted a vegetable garden.

Each Saturday he went to the village—sometimes with his cart, pulled by his oxen, to deliver goods to the local consortium; other times by bicycle, simply to purchase tobacco. While there he would pay a visit to the barber, hoping to find as many clients as possible so that he would have time to leaf through the magazines and newspapers in an attempt to keep minimally informed about what was happening in the world.

The locals never managed to establish any form of relationship with him; he limited his interactions with the director of the consortium and the tobacconist to a mumbled *"Buongiorno."* Curiously, his barber, whom he patronized for years, was Poppo, one of the men who had assaulted him outside the bar during the war. He held no rancor towards him as he had always considered him a dupe (as, in fact, did the entire village); Ultimo forgave him because his affiliation with the *squadristi* had been an act of weakness, and he had been visibly dominated by the company he kept. Ultimo told me that for all the time Poppo shaved him, the moment he passed his blade over the scar on his cheek, he would tremble slightly; and though he was a client for over thirty years, not once did they exchange a single word. After rising from the chair Ultimo would take the exact change from his pocket and leave it on the counter, then collect his hat, replace his cape on his shoulders, and depart in silence.

Ultimo, despite his hermetic existence, certainly did look after his appearance; in fact I found him a bit of a dandy, almost conceited. It was this paradox, among his many others, that made him so intriguing to everyone's eyes: despite his gruff ways he had a gentle aspect, and while he lived an anchoritic life his turquoise eyes and beaming smile seemed a kind of invitation. It was perhaps inevitable that he ignited the fantasies of many women, but he never gratified any. His first and only act of love was that passionate encounter with Elena in the summer of '44, which had resulted in Vittoria.

The scar on his otherwise beatific face gave him the aspect of a hero, and a kind of mythology sprang up about him. The younger generation in particular attributed to him a multitude of valiant feats that in reality he had never performed. To listen to the gossip, you'd have thought he single-handedly defeated the Nazi-Fascists and liberated Chianti; and his capture and unexpected return at the end of the war remained legendary in the talk of the town. Hundreds of inferences and far-fetched speculations persisted, but no one had ever come close to the truth of his internment in Auschwitz, for he kept the brand on his wrist well hidden. But he was undoubtedly the only living person in the area who had soiled his hands with an act of blood, and this elevated him to a grave and fearsome status; it was whispered that he had strangled and sent to hell an ominous tyrant in order to save his mentally ill sister from sexual assault.

Ultimo went about his life without much awareness of the mutations of the village in the post-war era and through the national economic expansion of the 1950s, nor of the tumult of the '60s, the terrorism of the '70s, or the decades that led into the new millennium. He remained attached to his world of the beginning of the century, and was indifferent to the revolutions in technology and travel. His only departures from Chianti were his deportation to Poland and a very few visits to Siena. He had never seen the sea, despite my having invited him to accompany me on numerous occasions. He had never been to Rome or even Florence. For a hundred years, he had lived on the *Macie,* cultivating the lands and immersing himself in the history of those who preceded him. I personally considered him an accomplished man, living a full life. And while that life seemed at first glance to be his choice, on reflection it became clear that destiny had ordained it for him.

Ultimo was concerned about how I lived my own life and often asked about my work. Each time I travelled abroad, it was for leisure or to conduct a book tour around the world; he listened with interest, but without envy. He observed me with that vaguely dreamy look I knew so well, his forehead furrowed. He encouraged me, after two decades, to abandon the tour-guide profession he had pointed me to, and pursue instead my writing, as that was now the manner in which I might most effectively share my love of Chianti. When I began to achieve some recognition and even renown, I sent him my newspaper reviews, which he absorbed with satisfaction. He always demanded not to be mentioned by me, not even in the appendix or acknowledgments, despite the fact that I owed him so much; he had so generously and unselfishly bestowed on me his wisdom, experiences, resources, and advice, without which I would never have achieved anything.

It was when we returned to the *Macie* on the evening of the seventh day after our departure, that he announced his decision to limit my visits to one a month, which caused me extreme distress. I could not understand his reasons; we were now so close, closer than ever. Looking back, I now realize that we may have been too close. Seeing me now was, perhaps, a bit like confronting the brand on his wrist.

Chapter 48

11ᵗʰ of October 2008

Waking up in a comfortable bed with a firm roof over my head, after two bumptious nights at the bivouac, I felt rested and full of vigor. My mood was considerably lightened. The sun was streaming through the window, and only a slight haze lurked at the foot of the valley, imparting that distinctive touch of fall.

And yet I was hesitant as to what to do. There were two possibilities: I could continue south till I reached Castelnuovo in the evening. From there I could hop on a bus back to my village. The alternative was to return the way that I'd come, by the route Ultimo had taught me. I decided to postpone the decision till after breakfast.

As in the old days, this began with the stale bread in my knapsack. I sliced it, doused it with red wine, then sprinkled it with sugar I found in a tin on one of the shelves. Then I sat on the veranda, my feet resting on a table just like successful managers would do. Contemplating the vistas while the sun warmed my neck, I leafed through a book I'd found inside that described rural life during Roman times. A pair of lizards skittered under the table, drawing my attention from the text. Their jerking movements reminded me of the clockwork animation of old tin toys one wound up with a key.

Returning to the text, I realized that most of the passages by Cato, Varro, Plinio and Columella were referring to this very part of Tuscany, as their descriptions of the landscapes were identical to what was at this moment sprawled out before me. While I contemplated the timeless beauty, my heart suddenly jumped; for there was now a human figure coming out of the woods. Despite the distance I could distinguish it as female, because of the sinuous gait. I lowered the book to the adjacent table and watched her approach.

When she was close enough to be able to see clearly, I was astonished to note that she was clad in antiquated though elegant robes. When she was but a few yards away, she raised her hand to greet me. I politely got to my feet and returned the gesture, though with less sweeping grace than my newly arrived guest, for I was astonished at this sudden visitation.

Chapter 49

11th of October 2008 - Tanaquilla

She had wide, tenebrous eyes of dark brown. Her wavy, raven-black hair was collected in a chignon cinched by a net that dropped to just above her shoulders. When she turned, the linen of her ivory tunic made a rustling sound, and I could see that her nose was prominent and noble, typical of a Greek profile. When she gestured, her splendid ornaments tinkled and sang: diadems, earrings, bracelets, rings, fibulas in bronze, silver, gold and electrum.

"You must be Dario," she said with a hint of wry amusement, devoid of any shyness.

"I am," I said, guardedly. "With whom do I have the pleasure of speaking?" I stuttered a bit, unable to ascertain whether I was the victim of a very well-organized prank.

"My name is Tanaquilla. Ultimo alerted me to your arrival. Welcome!"

I grunted, unable to speak, completely stupefied.

She gave the slightest pout. "Hadn't Ultimo told you about me? How very ungallant of him." She then smiled enigmatically. "I have a few errands I must perform, after which I will return. In the meantime, I leave you with some freshly baked bread."

I grunted again, even more stunned to see set before me a straw basked covered by a beige cloth. I hadn't noticed her carrying it before.

Tanaquilla lowered herself into a chair with sublime elegance. I saw that she wore sandals, the tips of which curled skywards; they had a wooden base with a central joint that permitted her to bend her feet. Suddenly I had the entirely irrational, yet inescapably certain idea that this was an authentic Etruscan woman, and the more I looked at her the more convinced I became. She had all the distinguishing traits and characteristics I'd learned under Ultimo's tutelage.

Her luminescent countenance was adorned by makeup made from clay, ochre, earth, and talcum; her eyes were set off by a green malachite powder, the eyelids embellished with a pink amalgamation mixed from minerals and oils; and her lips were sharply lined in crimson acquired from the soil, and known as *Milton.* Unlike myself, Tanaquilla appeared perfectly at ease in the company of someone more than two millennia removed from her own time.

She produced a rectangular wooden *ciste* (essentially a beauty case), decorated with leather and inlaid with ivory, gold, and silver, and nonchalantly set it on the table before her. She opened it and pulled out a goose-shaped *askos* from which she extracted two drops of pine and myrtle perfume, which she casually applied to her neck, the rings on her fingers glinting in the sun.

I watched her perform these ablutions with some embarrassment; the intimacy of the act added to the general surreal nature of the visit. My jaw still hung on my chest; I strove to collect myself, to find something to say. I settled on asking what her errand was, and when she would return here to the barn I had come to know as *La Speranza.*

With the kind of regal poise any contemporary woman would envy, she looked directly at me with her phenomenal eyes and said, "I owe a visit to my *thuva* and his *puia*; my brother Varna and his wife Ramtha. Tomorrow they hold a banquet in honor of the god Tinio. Varna recently returned from the devastation of Cuma, miraculously unscathed. It was a great defeat for our people, but we feel compelled to pay homage to Tinio for having spared him."

I reached back into my memories. The great sea battle of Cuma was fought in 474 B.C. between the Etruscan and the Syracusan fleets, the latter commanded by Ierone I. With this victory the Greeks put an end to the expansion of the Etruscans in southern Italy, and struck a terrible blow to the political influence they wielded in the Italian peninsula.

Tanaquilla watched me as if waiting for comment. I didn't want to reveal to her that the defeat unfortunately marked the decline of her people, so I changed the subject. "It sounds like a fine feast, Tanaquilla; have you decided what to cook?"

Again she smiled, and ran her hand over her hair; her metallic bracelets jangled. "We will roast a swine," she said, "and serve cereal soups and vegetables prepared by *ati nacna*—my grandmother. There will also be boiled chicken accompanied by scallions and garlic. Before the banquet, the priestess will spill some wine in honor of Tinio, while a *clan*—or son—or one of the invited will play the lyre."

I tried to imagine the banquet hall. The wooden fittings of the noble families would be painted with vibrant colors and were essentially tables, benches and couches, the latter possibly made of wicker. The walls would be richly decorated with frescoes and hung with totems and charms for good fortune. The most commonly used utensils would be the incense burners, cisterns, mobile braziers, bronze candle bearers, and figures fashioned from terracotta, tin and copper.

The Etruscans had also possessed abundant crockery, plates, cups and jugs in *bucchero* (a black-clay ceramic polished on the surface) and in the richer homes, even in bronze, silver and gold. Axes and skewers were used to chop meat that was then roasted on apposite braziers and tripods, while pitchers, jars, and jugs were used to serve wine and oil. Servants served the food and drink while those in attendance dined while reclining on their sides.

I observed Tanaquilla and concluded that she was indeed a splendid Etruscan matron; emancipated and uninhibited, with an almost maniacal care of her appearance. I was bewildered that she actually sat before me with her shapely legs crossed as though it were the most normal thing in the world. What on earth was going on? She took a quick glance at the book I'd set on the table and said, "What are you reading?" When I replied that it was a text on Roman rural life, she turned her head away and waved in dismissal. This was to be expected; a decent Etruscan had no sympathy for Roman culture.

One noted difference between the Greek and Roman worlds was that Etruscan women were granted almost complete liberty. For the Latins, however, women were to be *lanifica et domiseda,* meaning that they should stay at home, devote themselves to weaving, and let the *pater familias* (the head of the family) lay down the law, including the infliction of punishment—which might mean death for even the most trivial offences, such as drinking wine. Etruscan women, on the other hand, were free to take part in convivial banquets, share the same *kline* (bed) as their men, and participate in sporting competitions and theatrical entertainments. In the upper classes they were even permitted to pass their family names on to their children. The Romans found this scandalous and didn't hesitate to stigmatise Etruscan women as licentious and possessed of loose morals. The term "Etruscan woman" became synonymous with prostitute. But the social condition of Etruscan females was unique in the panorama of the Mediterranean world, and possibly this is evidenced by the different lineage of the populations: pre-Indo-Europe-an attributed to the Etruscans, Indo-Europeans to the Latin and Greeks.

Tanaquilla suddenly interrupted my reverie by saying, "Very well then, Dario, I'm off." She stood up, adjusted her tunic, collected her *cistis* and sashayed off as though she were on the catwalk at a high-couture fashion show in Milan. Her flowing tunic danced in the wind, and she trailed fascination and charm with each step. Just prior to dissolving from my visual field, she turned and called out, "Make sure to start the fire; I'll be back soon. In the meantime, meditate. Even in your veins flows Rasna blood—or the blood of the Etruscans, as you insist on calling us." Then she gave a little wave and was gone.

I sat for a while in utter bafflement. By some uncanny means I had just made the acquaintance of a woman who had lived here roughly 2,450 years earlier. It was clear to me that either Ultimo's hand was in this, or the well water contained some psychotropic drugs. Of the two possibilities, the first was by far the more plausible.

Chapter 50

11th of October 2008

Alone again, I felt myself reeling. I couldn't think what to do. Tanaquilla had asked that I start the fire, but it seemed bizarre to act on the request of someone who might very well be an apparition. But for lack of any better plan, this is what I resorted to. I then placed the wicker basket with the bread she'd given me inside the walnut kneading trough.

Once the fire was blazing and no longer required my tending, I went back outside and scrutinized the hilly vistas of Chianti. Suddenly the long country hikes I had taken in Ultimo's company came rushing back from over the years, and I recalled how he took those opportunities to illustrate for me the seductive history of these lands. The Etruscans, I learned from him, were the first civilized population in Chianti and asserted a strong influence. Before them there had been only the primitive Villanovians, a nomadic people who had moved along the rivers and lived almost exclusively by breeding sheep.

Descending into the surrounding valleys, I bent over and picked up a tiny fragment of cobbled surface that had probably paved the path I was treading. In fact the small, forgotten roadway, now overgrown with weeds, was none other than the ancient Cassia, and in my hand I was holding a shard of pavement from what had once been one of the most famous highways in the Roman world. I turned it repeatedly in my hand and then directed my gaze toward the Berardegna valleys; there in the distance I spotted the *Colonna del Grillo,* where thousands of years ago a group of Greek merchants had settled. From there, the road ascended and lapped the agglomerations marked on the Roman maps, all of which still exist today; they were known by the names of Ponticelli, Petrosa, Sexta, Chinicciano, Tisciano, and so on, all the way up to Pieve Asciata where in those times had stood an inn. The road then passed through my village of Vagliagli and continued to Fonterutoli and Castellina in Chianti, where it dovetailed into another main road.

The Romans, however, never really held Chianti in any particular regard, given that it was a rocky and unyielding area. Despite this they often travelled through here, as it made for a more direct route and was also decidedly more favorable than moving through the swampy lowlands, where the risk of malaria was high.

I sat and sighed, realizing that my walks with Ultimo would never recur; and that from now on I would gaze contentedly on these hills alone, as indeed I was doing now. I missed so much attending his words, though I was grateful to have been, in many ways, his apprentice, or pupil for so long.

From my vantage point I could see visible traces of the ancient road that would have conducted the Celts, headed by Brennus, to sack Rome, and where it is said his army camped—a location that was not by chance named Brenna.

Even the Lombards in the 6th century had passed through here on their warlike peregrinations southward, some settling here permanently. Curiously, despite their being well known as a spiteful and cruel people, they mixed peacefully with the few indigenous natives who were converted to Christianity and created a new race that was the result of this commingling of Scandinavian and Mediterranean blood. The mix is evident in any local village where fair hair and blue eyes coexist beside darker, swarthier features, with a majority—such as Ultimo and myself—exhibiting traits of both.

Turning my gaze to the west, on the opposite side of the valley, I could distinctly see where another essential road of the early epochs had been laid—one that surpassed the Cassia in importance: that being the Via Francigena that had been sought by Charlemagne. He erected numerous Romanesque abbeys that are still today fully active, while other churches that dotted my vision could be attributed to the knights Templar during the late Middle Ages.

Wherever my eyes fell I could pick out castles and towers erected over the course of the centuries, many during the battles between the Florentine Guelph and the Sienese Ghibelline armies, which raged for four hundred years; and right there, on that lower hill, on the 4th of September, 1260, they faced each other in a confrontation so brutal that Dante Alighieri immortalized it with the famous phrase: "The slaughter that dyed the river Arbia red with blood." The Florentine army had marched right where I was sitting and camped at Monteaperti. Headed by Jacopino Rangoni, they comprised some 3,000 horse and 30,000 troops, while the Sienese, commanded by Provenzano, were only 17,000 infantry and 1,000 cavaliers. Despite this, Siena won a victory still celebrated today for its defiance of the odds. 10,000 Florentines were massacred and 15,000 taken prisoner, compared to 600 Sienese casualties and just over 400 captives.

Those battles continued without interruption in the succeeding centuries, until the fall of Siena in 1555 gave ultimate victory to the Florentine Republic, paving the way to an extended peace that fostered the Renaissance, or as Ultimo defined it, "Tuscan imperialism in the world." How could one not agree with him? In whatever direction I looked, I recognized locations that had once belonged to well-known persons who were either born or had lived in Chianti. For example, the great statesman and political philosopher Niccolò

Machiavelli was a native of Sant'Andrea in Percussina, not far from where I stood; Leonardo was born just miles away in Vinci and it seems most probable that he had painted the Mona Lisa at Villa Vignamaggio, just a stone's throw away from *La Speranza*. Michelangelo and even Galileo spent time here, being enthusiasts of the local wine, known as *vermiglio* in those years. Greve in Chianti gave birth to renowned navigators such as Amerigo Vespucci and Giovanni Verrazzano.

Then again, in the 18th century, the region suffered another invasion, by Napoleonic forces that sacked and sowed terror among the local populations. Directly before me I could see the majestic walls of Castle Brolio rising up; after a thousand years, it is still the property of the Ricasoli family, of which the most famous member not only created and launched Chianti wine in the world, but was one of the fathers of Unification, and was Prime Minister of the second Italian government in 1861-62 and again in 1866-67.

I felt favored by a fate that allowed me to live in these lands, so drenched by history and legend, and fortunate to be able to share and breathe this mysterious fairy tale atmosphere. My eyes dampened with happiness, though they were soon dried by the gentle breeze; yet nothing could quell the emotion I felt on remembering, again, my singular friend Ultimo. What, I asked myself, would my life have been like without him…?

Chapter 51

The return of Tanaquilla

I returned to *La Speranza* to find the hall enshrouded in warm smoke and the fire extinguished. I stoked it back to life by feeding the embers with some thin, dry oak branches from the stack of pinecones I'd collected beneath the imposing tree at the entrance of the woods. The sun was now setting behind the western hills and the air had turned crisp.

I filled my glass with red wine and sat on the wicker mat before the fireplace, watching as the flames regained their vigor. At that moment, Tanaquilla reappeared, startling me with her hushed step. Over her lined tunic she wore a coarse woollen cape, fixed to her shoulders with bronze fasteners. Almost as if to certify her disaffection for the Romans, she joined me in a glass of wine. Then, showing herself to be quite at home, she broke a piece from the wheel of seasoned pecorino cheese, topped it with a quince fruit paste, and placed it atop a fragrant *focaccia* stuffed with rosemary from the basket she'd left in my custody.

She sat next to me, cross-legged yet elegant. "Ultimo spoke to me of you often," she said. "He is an astonishing man. He worked for years to restore this place."

Again I felt the awkwardness of not knowing how to respond. I feared that to enter into such an intimate discussion might be too discordant; might it not break the spell?

But as usual Tanaquilla took charge of the situation, and after we'd finished our frugal meal she abruptly stood up and adjusted her tunic. "Ultimo intended that I reveal to you a secret," she said, and she took my hand, gently guided me to my feet, and led me away from the fire. My heart began thrumming, both from the excitement of touching this stunning, timeless beauty as well as from anticipation of what was next to occur.

"Can you see that opening?" she asked, pointing to the entrance to the cellar. When I nodded, she said, "It's actually a *tholos.*"

"A tomb?" I said, baffled. "But…do you realize what you're telling me?"

"Of course I do, Dario. It was dug out by my ancestors, as was this flight of stairs—this *dromus.* It was to hold the cinerary urn of Larth, the progenitor of the highly respected family to which I belong."

We descended, still hand-in-hand. No paintings were visible on the walls, nor were any of the usual fittings in evidence. I took up the torch and lit it, and illumination splashed all about the place.

The interior of tombs varied substantially, according to the economic standing of the proprietor, and this one consisted of a sole chamber, evincing the humble social extraction of the departed.

I had often visited Etruscan tombs belonging to noble families, and I was well aware of how they reproduced in minute detail the homes the departed had dwelled in. Doors and windows were usually framed in elegant casings, furniture and fittings were duplicated in carved rock. Interior windows providing a view into the adjacent rooms, were generally inserted into the walls dividing the cells. All around were stools, counters, couches with erect backrests, and beds with ornate supports. On the wall hung weapons, and scattered about the room were the various tools belonging to the deceased; everything combining to render the sepulchral home alive and throbbing.

The tomb was bare and small, but I was excited to be standing here, especially in the company of an Etruscan woman such as Tanaquilla, and gratified to know that it belonged to her forebear, a warrior of modest means.

"As you can see," she said in a respectful undertone, "someone had so little respect for him that the urn and his few personal effects have all been sacked. They were probably sold to an unscrupulous collector." We remained silent for a moment, and I felt a shiver of guilt, almost as though I were responsible for the profanation of the tomb.

Tanaquilla somehow intuited my feeling. "I'm certain Larth is smiling now, however, as he was a great lover of wine, and would be honoured that his tomb now serves as a cellar!" She was both gracious and wise, with a voice like the tinkling of bells. Then she turned to me and said, "Ultimo Gori is a direct descendant of my forefather Larth, and so consequently is my cousin. A distant one, of course, but a cousin all the same." I was too stunned to know how to reply. Silence again loomed; then Tanaquilla took the torch from me, and the light blazed momentarily across her uncanny countenance. She smiled and stroked my cheek with her impeccably manicured fingers. "I must go now. My family awaits me."

I followed her up the granite steps, watching the delicate sway of her hips, the pivot of her elbows as she drew her hood over her head, casting her face into darkness. When we reached the top of the stairs, she sailed over to the door. Then she waited, like a true noblewoman, for me to open it for her.

"Addio, Tanaquilla," I said. "Take care of yourself!"

"Addio Dario, it was an honor to make your acquaintance. Perhaps we shall meet again one day."

I accompanied her across the yard and watched as she receded, swallowed up by the tenebrous Chianti night. I returned to the *osteria*, still trying to determine whether or not I was truly awake, or lost in some vivid delusion. I pinched myself to see if I was dreaming; the sharp pain was tangible. Apparently I was awake.

I filled another glass with wine, then went upstairs and lay down on the bed. My thoughts returned to Ultimo. I would never be able to thank him for this final gift he had bestowed on me—and I might never know exactly how he managed to accomplish it.

Chapter 52

12th of October 2008 - Melchiorre

My sleep was interrupted by a racket coming from outside. I stirred, expecting to find some faint morning light on opening my eyes, but it was still the jet-black depth of the night. I sat up and listened to the din, wondering what it could be; but it suddenly went quiet. I was just about to lay back down, when there came a violent bluster at the front door, as if someone had hurled his shoulders against it. Then came the sound of the tables and chairs on the patio being knocked about like tenpins.

My heart beating wildly, I pushed away the blanket and lurched barefoot to the window, and peered into the darkness, trying to discern the origin of all that clamor. And there in the murk of night I could just see him: a large orb of white, careening through the pitch. It was Melchiorre, the albino wild boar. As if sensing my presence, he now stood still and gazed up at me from below. It was almost as though he had been trying to draw my attention.

I flew down the stairs, completely naked and at risk of stumbling in the dark, and threw open the door. Melchiorre trotted over to me and rested his wet snout in my outstretched hand. His red eyes were expressive and bright in the starlight, and he emitted a series of feeble grunts, as though trying to communicate something to me. I stroked his bristly white cloak for an instant, before he jerked away and ran back towards the woods.

Before entering the cover of the foliage he stopped; the lunar luminosity danced across his snow-white fur. He turned his head as though inviting me to follow, then scraped the ground with his hooves and plunged into the flora.

By some strange telepathy I knew that I must abandon the *osteria* and return to the *Macie*. I hastily dressed and collected my things, realizing that something ominous had occurred to Ultimo; and I decided to return by the shorter route. I needed half a day to reach San Gusmè on foot, and from there I could hop on the first public bus back to my village, where I could pick up my old Vespa and reach the *Macie* by evening.

I arrived in San Gusmè at lunchtime and learned that a bus would depart only in a few hours. So to kill time and distract my thoughts from Ultimo, I waited in a *trattoria* where I ordered a plate of homemade *pici* and a rosemary flavored *tagliata*. But the distraction didn't work. My mind kept wandering back to my old friend, and I worried at how I might find him.

That night I rattled up to the *Macie* in much the same way I arrived the first time, so many years before. And as before I parked the old Vespa against the wall of Ultimo's barn; there was little risk of it impeding him now.

I leapt up the steps as I'd done thousands of times over the years. The door was ajar and I gently pushed it open. The house was in perfect order, but even from here I could see that Ultimo's bedroom was wide open, and the bed empty and recently made.

There had never been a phone in that house and I still didn't own a mobile. As the sun was setting I felt it wise to remain there. I settled down on the couch. In the morning I would go to the village in search of information. Strangely, I suffered no more anxiety; spending the night beneath Ultimo's roof—and lulling myself to sleep with a glass of his wine—it seemed, in a way, that I had already found him.

I slept soundly until I was briskly shaken awake; and when I opened my eyes, I found myself being regarded by a familiar countenance. Clad in an elegant double-breasted jacket and leaning on a walking stick, the old gentleman smiled at me from beneath his well-manicured mustache. It was Lorenzo.

Chapter 53

13ᵗʰ of October 2008 - A Dream?

Lorenzo smiled, revealing two gold-capped teeth. He was exactly as I'd recalled him from our first and only encounter, though his nose was now cross-hatched by traces of burst blood vessels. He removed his Borsalino hat while I pulled myself up to a sitting position.

"Dario," he said, "how nice to see you again. Thank you for delivering my letter; I'm sorry it took me so long to say so, but when I gave it to you I had but a few months to live. However because of you I at last obtained his pardon, and consequently I was able to depart this world in peace. Now please, follow me, but in silence, I beg you!" He emphasized this last point by putting two fingers over his lips.

He opened the door to Ultimo's living room. The immense fireplace was burning sufficiently to light up the whole place. The refectory table was essentially bare but for a flask of wine and some clay mugs. And milling about everywhere were people, silhouetted against the fire and the oil lamps. At one end of the table sat a bald man I knew at once to be Gosto, and next to him his wife Annita, her hair pulled back into a long pigtail. I distinguished Virginia, with Tosca on her lap, and Armido playing the accordion from inside the hearth while Adelmo cavorted in a lumpish dance. Delfino added harmony with his mouth organ, while his fiancé Lucia clapped the time and Ricciotti, seated on the table, juggled onions like a jester.

Primo was silent in the darkest corner, while Tancredi, in uniform, beat his foot to the rhythm of the tune, causing the medals on his chest to twinkle in the firelight. Giuseppina— the beautiful *Pina l'Etrusca*—cooed a lullaby to baby Maria Pia, who clung lovingly to her breast. Antonia scribbled abstract designs on the interior of the fireplace, looking cross whenever Adelmo blocked her light, while Carlotta pirouetted around the room, her honey-colored hair bouncing loosely on her shoulders.

At the opposite end of the table sat a man with his back to us; he seemed to feel my eyes upon him, for he now turned to look at me. It was a rejuvenated Ultimo, his hair dark and his face unlined and his cheek unscarred. When he caught my eye he grinned happily, raised his chalice towards us, and winked. Then he turned back to those he had long loved, and lost, and now loved again.

Chapter 54

Annita

I was still enraptured by the beautiful vision of Lorenzo and the Gori family reunited before the fireplace when I was roused by the sound of the door unbolting. The room seemed to shimmer with light and freshness, and framed in the doorway I saw the silhouette of a woman. I drew myself up to attention. When the door closed, leaving only the light of the room, I recognized the arrival as she who had been nursing Ultimo the last time I'd been here, just a few days before, and who had left me the message calling me to his side. I stood up from the couch, covering my nakedness with a rug. She seemed unfazed by my presence; in fact she seemed preoccupied by sorrow.

"I returned last night from an errand for Ultimo," I explained. I nodded my head towards his now-empty bedroom. "But I'm too late to tell him. He has died, hasn't he?" My throat constricted with emotion, so that I had to choke out the words, "I would like to accompany him to the cemetery."

The woman, who I now realized reminded me amazingly of Tanaquilla, approached and embraced me; and with her fetching American intonation, she said, "Ultimo vanished two days ago. The *Carabinieri* have been searching for him far and wide, but haven't had any luck. Do you have any idea where he might be? You should, you know him so well." The moment she completed the phrase, she tightened her grip and started sobbing into my chest.

Chapter 55

Epilogue

Ultimo's body was not found; it was for me an unequivocal certainty that it never would be. Knowing him, I was certain the last thing he desired was to be interred and mourned in a cemetery. He was an essential and vital part of Chianti and, like the Native Americans, or the wild animals with whom he shared such a rapport, he preferred to end his existence in some private place, under an open sky, that I was sure he had chosen many years ago.

I spent the remainder of that morning in the company of the woman, who introduced herself as Annita Terrosi—the first name a reflection of her great-grandmother, the second inherited from her step-grandfather. She was Ultimo and Elena's granddaughter, through their daughter Vittoria. Annita had moved to the village eleven years before and, entirely unbeknownst to me, had cared for Ultimo during the waning years of his life. She knew precisely who I was, for Ultimo had told her all about our relationship; but he had never uttered a word about her to me.

We began seeing each other occasionally over the succeeding weeks and months; then with more frequency and attentiveness; and suddenly a deep friendship blossomed. Each time I looked at her I was reminded of Tanaquilla; but this wasn't so bizarre as she, too, bore that lady's noble blood. Annita had always longed to visit Chianti, the land of her roots, but had been kept in the dark about the vicissitudes suffered by the Gori family. When she turned eighteen, Lorenzo told her only that her mother, Vittoria, was not his biological daughter, but had been fathered by a friend who had once saved his life.

She never knew her own father, who abandoned Vittoria before she was born, and grew up living with her mother and grandparents, in a house where by rule only Italian was spoken. She graduated with a degree from UCLA and when she inherited the apartment in Tuscany and obtained Italian citizenship, she decided to move here permanently and found a job as a high school teacher in Siena.

Over time I learned that she was a paradoxical creature, sweet-natured and self-assured, yet devoted to solitude. We fell into the habit of taking long rides on our bicycles and epic hikes through the Chianti hills, and after a few months, when the warmth of our relationship hadn't waned, I decided she should accompany me to *La Speranza*—the *Osteria* in Chianti.

During the long ramble, I shared with her the entire history of Ultimo and Lorenzo, just as Ultimo had done with me. She listened attentively, absorbing the story; and showed her heritage by having no problem at all adapting to rough-and-tumble bivouacs and nights spent in shelters half-reclaimed by nature. We never caught sight of Melchiorre, but the little fox, Baldassarre, appeared unexpectedly to us on the platform of the tree where we spent one night, and followed us when we departed, keeping a certain distance until, after several miles, he got bored with us and trotted away.

Annita immediately adored *La Speranza,* but when I told her all about my encounter with Tanaquilla there, she didn't believe me. How could I blame her?...And yet we were visited by another presence during our time there. Our deep affection gave way at last to passionate love, and in the bedroom that Ultimo had created in the loft, we conceived a daughter, whom we named Lorenza.

Annita and I decided to move our new family to the *Macie,* which she had inherited, and I became a winemaker, though I did not abandon my passion for writing.

One evening upon returning from the vineyards, I lifted my eyes skywards, scrutinizing carefully the meek, milky clouds as they dappled the atmosphere. The rosy luminescence of twilight flooded my venerated hills with a portentous and refractive light. My bond with Ultimo had been resolutely and indivisibly sealed, for now I myself had become an integral part of the descendants and lineage of Larth.

2008

2008, according to the Ab Urbe Condita calendar, was 2761; for the Chinese, 4704/05; in the Jewish calendar it was 5767/68, in the Vikrama Samvat Hindu calendar 2063/64, in the Shaka Samvat calendar 1930/31; the Kali Yuga calendar gave it as 5109/10. The Persian calendar denoted it as 1386/87, the Islamic calendar 1429/30; in the Byzantine calendar it was 7516/17, and for the Berbers 2958; the Runic calendar showed it as 2258. According to the Gregorian calendar it was MMVIII, and also a leap year.

The UN proclaimed 2008 the international year of the planet; the Palladian year marked 2008 as the fifth centenary of the birth of architect Palladio, and the Vatican dedicated the Pauline Year to Apostle Paul, celebrated the bimillenium of his birth. The Euro became the official currency in Cyprus and Malta.

According to Chinese astrology, 2008 ended the Year of the Pig and initiated the Year of the Mouse, while in Italy, early elections were called. The President of the Italian Republic was Giorgio Napolitano and the Prime Minister was Silvio Berlusconi, serving a third term of office. In Siena, the July Palio was won by the Istrice (Porcupine) Contrada with the jockey Trecciolino and the horse Già del Menhir, while the August Palio was won by the Bruco (Caterpillar) Contrada with Gingillo on Elisir de Lugodoro.

Zaragoza hosted the International Expo. The asteroid 2008 BT18 passed close to planet Earth. In Tokyo, a groundbreaking celebration was held for the Tokyo Sky Tree; Sydney hosted the 23rd World Youth Day; and in Beijing, the 29th Olympics took place.

Between March and April, the increase in the price of

wheat and rice provoked tensions and revolts in different parts of the world, including Egypt, Thailand, Cameroon, and the Ivory Coast. Stock markets collapsed all over the world causing huge losses. Water was discovered on Mars; Fidel Castro announced his resignation as President and head of the military forces of Cuba. Ten thousand Turkish soldiers invaded Kurdistan in northern Iraq. Dmitrij Medvedev in Russia was backed as a candidate by Valdimir Putin and won an easy victory.

In Lhasa in Tibet, the Chinese army put a bloody end to a demonstration by Buddhist monks. In Great Britain the Labour party collapsed. With the Georgian occupation of southern Ossezia and the consequent Russian reaction, the Ossezian war commenced. The failure of Lehmann Brothers provoked an additional worldwide financial crash. The Israelis raided the Gaza strip. Jean-Marie Gustave Le Clézio was awarded the Nobel prize in literature. Senator Barack Obama was elected as 44th President of the United States of America.

In 2008, Mt. Everest's conqueror Sir Edmund Hillary died, as did chess player Bobby Fischer, actors Heath Ledger, Paul Newman, Roy Scheider, Richard Widmark, Sydney Pollack and Charlton Heston; also departed were sculptor and painter Pietro Cascella, Indonesian former President Suharto, film director Dino Risi, stylist Yves Saint Laurent, singer Bo Diddley, the tenor Giuseppe Di Stefano, writer Tancredi Rigoni Stern, racing driver Phil Hill, pianist Richard Wright, Austrian politician Joerg Haider, businessmen Frank Rosenthal and Andrea Pininfarina, authors Barrington John Bayley and Michael Crichton, artist George Brecht, and model Bettie Page…

………. and in 2008 Ultimo Gori chose to depart this world. His body was never found.

Ringraziamenti

First of all, I wish to thank Diana, who believed this was a good book and helped consistently with the editing as well as having the patience to listen to me read it aloud to her before the fireplace on my birthday. My appreciation to Barbara with whom I jogged around the Siena fortress during the winter months, boring her with my narration of what I had written the day before; I owe her a dinner. Also thanks go to Ilaria who astonishingly devoted her college thesis to one of my books; and to Lucia, Debora, Elena, Roberta, Rosy, Francesca, Maria Renèe, Brenda, Annalisa, Elena, Lucia, Maya, Elissena, Agnese, Westcott, Joanne, Carolina, Elizabeth, Rochelle, Marta, and Tea.

All of the passionate *Contradaioli* of the Bruco Contrada have my gratitude, in particular Rettore Fabio, Capitano Gianni, Presidente Giorgio, *Zio* Massimo and Camilla, Gigi, Paolino, Katina, Kationa, the Falchi brothers, Francesco, Andrea, Beatrice, Claudia, Luciano, Marco, Claudio and a special *grazie* to my Bruco *madrina*, Luigina. All the inhabitants of my village, especially Michele and Maria Pia, Licia, Gregorio, Sara, Gnagno, Vincenzo, Maria, Francesca and Sara, my neighbors Massimo, Meris, Angelo, Domenico, Tonia, Beppe, Aurelia, Monica and Elvira. Sincere thanks go to my *socio,* Stefano.

My thanks go as well to my American manager, Laura, and her daughter, Esther Rose, my agent Allan and my Italian agents Letizia and Roberta, my parents Biancastella and Giovanni, my brother Cristiano and his wife Danda, and my nephews Anastasia, Sebastiano and Nicholas. Thanks to all the thousands who send me e-mails and to whom I endeavor to respond. Thanks to all those Americans who host me on my long book tours around the U.S. And of course, a huge *grazie* to Rob and Jeff (Goffredo). An extremely special grazie goes to James Swift for his editing and precious suggestions.

Ultimately, I wish to dedicate my thanks to an unknown man whose face inspired me to write this book, even if he will forever be unaware of this.

Indice

Finito di stampare nel mese di maggio 2010
per conto di Lorenzo Barbera Editore Srl
presso L.E.G.O., Lavis TN